Joe Richardson

Illustrated by
Roisin Bradley

First published in the UK in 2023.

Belkenny Publishing

British library cataloguing is available.

ISBN 978-1-7391429-2-6

For more information visit: www.theanimalinamy.com

For Nicola

x

Tarabally Town Tribune

WHERE ARE THE MISSING SCHOOL CHILDREN?

FIVE NOW MISSING!

In the west of the city, the Greater Spring Rock area woke up today to the shocking news that five children have now vanished without a trace.

All children, with ages ranging from four years old to eleven, have fallen victim to a set of highly skilled kidnappings.

Inspector Gilliland commented, 'The police are doing all they can to retrieve the children and bring the culprits to justice.

Patrols have been increased throughout all local areas, and a curfew will be enforced. Please remain vigilant. Those who witness any suspicious activity should contact their local station.

Henry McKeown (6), the latest victim was taken from his home late last night while both parents slept soundly just next door.

Like the four prior victims, Henry was taken from his bedroom with no signs of forced entry or exit.

Only one clue is common across all kidnappings, a mirror in each victim's bedroom was burnt black and scorched.

1
Box of Mirrors

It had just gone 3:30pm in Tarabally Town and already most curtains were drawn. The roads were quiet and the playparks empty. In the air hung an eerie stillness; the cold winter sun itself only dared peak occasionally in between the gaps in the rows of terraced houses.

Jamie swerved as his Mum extended her arms and moved in for a hug.

"Mum," he grunted, anxiously looking around.

Usually, he'd walk to Amy's house alone, but these were changed times; children were pulled a little closer and commutes were made much quicker. Seeing his friend's house in sight, he made a break for it. The streetlights, already on, threw shadows in front and then behind as he raced ahead.   The tail of his shirt flailed behind him, wild and free, matched only by his untamed dark hair that stuck out like the bristles of a chimney sweep brush.

Jamie gave his mum a quick, reassuring wave once he reached Amy's. Sweaty and panting, he withdrew the newspaper from his school bag and began frantically banging on the door.

Knock! **Knock!**

Nobody answered.

Knock! He hit on the door harder still, hurting his knuckles in the process.

Finally, it slowly swung open.

"What's the emergency, lad?" asked an elderly man. "Ahh, I see, the newspaper. Thank you. But next time, please display a little patience; I can't move as quickly as I used to." Taking the newspaper from Jamie, he went to close the door.

"Wait! You're not Amy!"

"What gave it away?" smiled the old man.

"Well, the grey hair did it first. Then there's the fact that you're a bit older than her. Oh, and you're probably twice as tall. I mean, how tall are you?" Jamie asked, looking up at the man.

"You must be young Jamie, I presume?"

Jamie just nodded, still open-mouthed and marvelling at the man's height.

"I'm Amy's grandfather...."

"Charlie," interrupted Jamie. "Where's Amy, though?"

"She's up in her room, been up there a while, doing yoga, I believe."

"Yoga?" questioned Jamie in a high-pitched tone. "But isn't that for old peop...I mean, isn't yoga for people who can't move around too well?"

Grandad Charlie hobbled backwards, revealing a walking stick and allowed Jamie into the house.

Jamie scanned the room, desperately looking at everything and anything but Grandad, "Ahh...I think I'll just keep quiet now and go on upstairs."

"Yeah, that might be best," smirked Grandad.

Jamie darted upstairs, taking them in twos, only to freeze when he noticed a peculiar handwritten sign on Amy's door that read: *'Silence when you enter!'*

He gently tapped on the door and tentatively walked in. The sound of waves crashed over him, and then the clicks and whistles of what he assumed were whales shocked him into a stationary pose. Centred in the room, Amy was curled up in a ball with her knees on the ground.

"Amy, have you seen..."

"Sshhhhh."

"But the newspaper, I think that...."

"Sshhhh," she repeated. "This is the Galapagos tortoise pose. They can live for almost 150 years. Probably because they are so relaxed and don't get interrupted during yoga." She smiled and took a long deep breath. The smart speaker on the cabinet beside her bed began counting down.

"5, 4, 3, 2, 1. Take a long deep breath. Hold it, perform the elephant pose, and release."

Amy stood up. She spread her legs shoulder width apart, placed one arm by her side and reached for the sky, stretching up like an elephant's trunk with the other.

The smart speaker continued to count her breathing.

"We don't have time for this, Amy," announced Jamie, pulling the plug from the wall.

"Hey, I need to do this. It's helping with managing my emotions. Otherwise, I could reveal an ability at any moment. And I can't, especially now Grandad is here."

"Well, it might be a good thing that he's here. We'll need all the help we can get because she's back, Amy! She's back!"

"Who's back?" replied Amy.

"Who do you think? Miss Quinn!"

"Impossible, Jamie. She wouldn't dare. As my parents said, we've seen the last of her." Amy reached down behind her bed to plug the speaker back into the wall.

"Haven't you seen the newspaper?"

"No, why? What does it say?"

Jamie went to reach into his bag before stopping, "Wait, your Grandad has it downstairs. But look, I'm telling you. She's back and she's up to her old tricks. Kidnapping kids again! Only this time, she's taking them from their beds!"

Amy closed her eyes and took a long deep breath in through her nose and out her mouth. "Come on; this isn't a comic or a movie. There's no sequel. I mean, how on earth could she possibly get in and out of a bedroom and not get caught?"

"Ahh ha, but think about it. She'd use the serum and turn herself into a mouse again. Then sneak into a house, inject a child, and then leave together. It's so unbelievably crazy that it might actually be brilliant."

Amy began slowly tracing her tongue around her lips and fiddled with a hairband around her wrist. "I think I need to see that newspaper. Grandad! Grandad!"

"Why all the shouting, Amy?" asked Mum, stumbling out of her room, weighed down with luggage. "Just go downstairs and talk to him. And here, take this with you."

Mum passed Amy a suitcase.

"What's this?" pressed Amy.

"Just the essentials for the rainforests of Costa Rica."

"Costa Rica? Who's going to Costa Rica?" interrupted Jamie, leaning over Amy's shoulder.

"Is that why Grandad's here? Are you serious?" added Amy incredulously.

"Watch the tone, young lady," sniffed Dad, coming out of the bedroom. "Here, Jamie, you can take this bag down for me. And relax, Amy, it's just me going."

"Sure, what's the worst that can happen when you leave?" began Jamie. "An old work colleague masquerades as a teacher, turns children into animals using serum, nearly kills your only daughter…and me! Steals your life's work and…"

"Okay, okay, I get the picture, Jamie. But I've got to go. They need me. Don't you know that a third of all the world's amphibian species are critically endangered?" replied Dad.

"Besides, I'm staying," smiled Mum. "And Grandad Charlie. So, there is no need to panic or stay with your cousins this time. Jamie can even stay over tonight; I've already sorted it with his mum."

"Well, I suppose that does help," Amy replied meekly.

"Best behaviour when I'm gone, please, you two. And Amy, keep those abilities in check."

"Oh, don't worry about us, Dad. We'll be a pair of angels."

Detecting the sarcasm dripping from his daughter's response, Dad grunted. "And remember, no abilities around Grandad."

"Doesn't he know?" spluttered Jamie.

"No, he doesn't," Dad replied sternly. "And it's going to stay that way."

"Listen, kids, I have to drop Dad at the airport, so I won't have time to cook. How does a Chinese takeaway sound?" said Mum spritely.

"Sounds good to me," smiled Jamie, grabbing a suitcase in each hand. "Let's get you two on the road."

*

No sooner had Mum and Dad's car left the driveway than the delivery of Chinese food arrived. Jamie, cradling the bag like a new-born baby, bolted through the sitting room and upstairs while Amy paused to study Grandad, sitting on the couch in peculiar silence, fixated on the newspaper.

"Can I have that, Grandad?" she asked, nodding towards the paper.

"After your dinner, Sweetheart. Now, get yourself upstairs and eat while it's hot. I'll explain everything later."

Explain everything?

The intrigued girl hadn't an appetite; Grandad was acting in an unusual way. He was too quiet, too still. *Did he know something? Was he reading the article about the missing children too?* He always made noise; when he cooked, read, or walked. Even his walking stick tapped a tune on the floor as he moved. If he wasn't humming or whistling, he was muttering to himself.

Amy darted into her room and snatched a bag of chicken balls from Jamie's hand.

"Grandad, fancy some food? We've got far too much," she yelled as she ventured downstairs.

"We don't, really," came a call behind her. "If he doesn't want them, then bring them back up. Bring some ketchup too."

But as she reached the last stair, Amy noticed the couch was empty. *Where was Grandad?* She held her breath and listened. Nothing. Only the sound of her heart beginning to pound faster in her chest. Then she saw that the mirror above the fireplace had been turned around to face the wall. *Strange.*

Suddenly Grandad emerged from the downstairs toilet carrying another mirror he had just ripped from the wall.

"Don't just stand there gawping, kiddo. We need to act fast. Grab the box I left in the kitchen and come on!"

Amy watched her grandfather slowly climb the stairs, using the handrail.

"What is the box for?"

"To put all the mirrors in," he yelled back, "the little ones. We can't miss any! We don't want to let them back in."

Let them back in? Bemused, Amy climbed the stairs, passing a rectangular stain where once a mirror had hung.

"Where's the box?" panted Grandad, "Look, never mind, take these." He dumped a pile of mirrors into Amy's arms, wiped the sweat from his brow and ambled off towards his granddaughter's room.

"Smells good, young man. Tell me, has Amy got any mirrors in here?"

With his two cheeks bulging like a hamster, Jamie pointed a curry-soaked finger towards the back of the door.

"Best keep it covered. Can't be too careful." Grandad threw a large towel over the mirror and marched back into the hall.

Jamie shrugged his shoulders and returned his focus to his dinner.

"What are you doing? Is Mum painting again?" asked Amy.

Mum had recently become obsessed with DIY shows on TV and was convinced she could do the same jobs at home by herself. The problem was that she never had a single lesson or even read a manual. She got all the help she needed online. However, she rarely watched any of the videos to the end. This led to some very questionable results. For instance, one light in the kitchen could turn on the kettle, ring the doorbell and even flush the downstairs toilet.

"No, Princess, she's not painting. It's for our

safety. We need to cover them, every single one of the mirrors!"

Princess! Urgh! Amy hated that term. She wasn't four years old.

Jamie joined her on the landing and stared as they watched Grandad shuffle into the bathroom next.

"You're in the spare room, aren't you?" Jamie asked Grandad as he returned with a small circular mirror. "Haven't you got any mirrors?"

"My room? No chance. Never use 'em, don't own one. They're only for vain people."

Amy thought for a moment, Grandad would regularly visit, and she'd never seen him use a mirror. She noted how his old camper van was missing rear-view and wing mirrors. She had never assumed that may have been on purpose.

The lack of mirrors might explain the tufts of grey hair on his face that he missed shaving, and it certainly explained his dress sense.

"But why do we need all the mirrors then?" she asked.

"Because they're close, Amy. Haven't you seen the news? This is the only way we can stop them coming in."

"They?" questioned Jamie. "You mean Miss Quinn has returned with backup?"

"It's not yer woman Quinn; she's long gone. I hear you two saw to that. No, no, this time, it's much more serious. They're coming in through the mirrors. That's how they snatch little kiddies!"

Amy rolled her eyes and sighed, "Of course, *they are*, Grandad. They're coming through the mirrors." She turned to go back to her room.

In entertaining his grandchild, Grandad often blurred the line between fiction and reality. This same man had pulled some whoppers in his time.

Most recently, he tried convincing his granddaughter that he had knocked down an alien while driving home from the supermarket. Grandad had a wickedly wild imagination, and while Amy enjoyed his tales, he often forgot that she is nearly twelve.

Grandad's withered old hand grabbed Amy's shoulder and pressed her. The old man spun her around and moved his face close. He stared intensely into her big blue eyes and, without blinking, whispered, "I've seen things that you can't imagine, things that cannot be unseen."

Amy gulped. It was hard and dry. She had never seen Grandad so spooked; he was usually the fun grandparent. To most, he appeared like a typical old person; he moved slowly, smelled a little and slept a lot, but not in Amy's eyes. To her, he was creative, brave, and endlessly selfless. Whatever Grandad had seen, or whatever he thought was coming, had his hands sweating and his body trembling.

"And I don't want you or any more kids to see what I have seen!"

"What have you seen?" Jamie asked, squeezing in between the pair.

"Beasts, my boy, there's a world in The Reflection filled with beasts."

Both children visibly shuddered.

Grandad went on, "We should keep all the mirrors away for now. At least for a few days, you know." His bushy grey eyebrows danced up and down, and his gravelly voice had a peculiar tone. Not the usual jolly tone when he spun a yarn.

He was serious, straight-faced and determined. He was almost desperate to convince the two wide-eyed children before him.

"We believe you, Grandad, but we need more details."

"Yeah, lots more details," added Jamie as he threw half a chicken ball into his mouth.

2
The Boy

Amy and Jamie followed Grandad downstairs and dumped all the mirrors into a box.

"Come on, spill the beans," urged Jamie. "You can't leave us hanging like that. We need info, and now!"

Thoughts in Amy's mind were circling round and round like a train on the tracks; a runaway train, without any stops, no words came out of her mouth quick enough. *Could there really exist a world of beasts inside the mirrors?*

"I shouldn't have told you anything. Look, just trust me when I say to cover all the mirrors. And not a word of this in front of your parents, that includes you too, Jamie. And would you look at the time," Grandad smiled. He dramatically yawned with a stretch. "Bedtime, I think. These old bones of mine need a good ten-hour kip. Details of The Reflection can wait until tomorrow; it's certainly not a tale one should share just before bed. But do me a favour and leave your door open a crack tonight, Darling." He kissed Amy's forehead and ruffled Jamie's hair.

Both children were left jittery, with wide eyes and knotted tummies.

The front door suddenly slammed shut, and Grandad paused at the foot of the stairs.

"Amy Sophia Cupples!" yelled Mum, kicking the box of mirrors by her feet. Amy only got her full name when she was being scolded. "What on earth is all this? Why are all my mirrors off the wall?"

"It wasn't me," began Amy. "Grandad took them down because…."

"You're painting," interrupted Grandad. "And by the look of the stains on the wall, they could do with a fresh lick. I'll tell you what, I'll even help while I'm here."

"We all will," added Jamie, winking to Grandad.

"Bed you two!" hissed Mum. "Now!"

The climb upstairs was much slower than usual. The missing mirrors made them uneasy. Even the Marvel posters Jamie gave Amy started to resemble someone climbing into the bedroom.

As Jamie settled down onto an airbed on the floor and Amy climbed under her animal duvet, the light spilling into the room did little to offer any comfort.

"He's joking, isn't he?" Jamie asked nervously. "I mean, a world inside the mirrors, ridiculous, isn't it?"

He hadn't taken his large brown eyes off the mirror and the towel that covered it.

"Yeah, ridiculous. It's got to be another one of his fantasies, doesn't it?"

"You don't seem convinced," added Jamie.

"Well, I haven't seen him like that before," replied Amy. "Taking mirrors down, sweating, panicking, and how he looked at me. It was all so real to him."

Staring at the covered mirror, her eyes grew narrow with suspicion and she bit her lower lip. It had to be an elaborate prank by Grandad, surely.

"There's only one thing for it!"

"Hot chocolate and forget the whole thing?" asked Jamie.

"Maybe, but first, I need to pull that towel off the mirror."

"I thought you might say that."

Tentatively Amy tip-toed across the thick carpet, stepping over clothes, dodging the empty Chinese food cartons and stood in front of the mirror. She held her breath. The only sounds were Jamie's panting and Grandad's snoring from next door. Slowly she raised her hands towards the mirror.

It moved!

The blood sank to her toes. Amy froze so abruptly that she forgot to breathe. Then with a frightful suddenness, she popped up from the ground and sprang across the room back into bed.

"Ah, Amy," whispered Jamie. "You might want to look at yourself, or maybe not. You've gone invisible."

Amy waved a transparent hand across her face.

"Breathe with me," began Jamie, searching for a hand to take hold of. "Deep breath in, hold, and breathe out. Good, good, that's it. You're already coming back. Ghost shrimp invisibility?" he quizzed.

Amy slowly nodded, never taking her eyes from the mirror.

"And the jump?"

"A flea," Amy replied. "Elastic in their joints. But Jamie, it moved! The towel moved!"

"What? How? Are you sure?"

"I'm telling you, a stick or something was pushing through the mirror." Amy cautiously rose to her feet and staggered forward.

"Wait! Get back here," grunted Jamie, pulling on the sleeve of her pyjamas. "What if it wasn't a stick? What if it was a claw or worse?"

Amy pressed on, dragging Jamie with her. She turned and nervously smiled. "Come on. We need to see that reflection."

Together they stood in front of the covered mirror. They looked at one another, took a deep breath, and then both reached out a hand and pinched the towel.

Five, four, three, Amy mouthed. Their hearts pounded in unison, two, one.

"A world inside the mirror, as if!" Amy stated with conviction.

In one rapid movement, they whipped the towel off to reveal the mirrored glass.

Then **WHOOSH!** A little silver ball no bigger than a marble whistled between their heads and whizzed around the room.

Moving as one, they jumped back into bed and cowered under the duvet. They could still hear the ball scream as it sliced through the air at unbelievable speeds. A blast of air shook the bed every time the little ball whipped past low and close. Then as quickly as it started, it stopped with a **clap!**

Trembling, Amy peeked out first to find herself staring directly at what looked like a boy. He stood proudly in the middle of the room with his clasped hands above his head. With a sudden jolt, he opened them. Startled, Amy shot back towards the wall. Jamie's intrigue saw him peek out just in time to see a cloud of dark dust delicately dance towards the ground.

Amy glanced towards the closed door and the mirror. The mirror! The towel lay on the floor. Her breathing shortened and accelerated, and the scream she willed to release was stuck in her throat.

"Relax, you two, you're safe now," smiled the boy.

Amy and Jamie resembled two stunned goldfish, gawping without speaking. *Was he from the mirror? Was he a kidnapper?*

"Ahh, you can breathe again."

"Who…who…are you? And what was…was…that?" stuttered Amy, puffing out her chest and edging in front of her trembling friend.

"It was an eyerie, but it didn't see anything," replied the boy. "Well, it's reflective dust now," he added, kicking the small pile at his feet.

"Reflective dust?" Amy repeated.

"And you're welcome, by the way."

"You're welcome?"

"Is there an echo in here?" smiled the stranger.

"Don't worry! I'm not here to hurt either of you."

Jamie's white knuckles still clutched the duvet as he leaned into Amy's ear. "Did he come from the…" he nodded towards the uncovered mirror.

"Speak up, Jamie. I can't hear you. What did he say, Amy?"

He knows our names!

"He wants to know if you came from the mirror?" asked Amy.

"The Reflection? I did, indeed. I had…"

"But you're not a beast. You're a boy," interrupted Jamie.

The mysterious figure stared at the pair of dumbstruck children and then began stuttering, "I'm….I'm….a boy? You mean a real-life boy?" He ran to the mirror and stared at himself. Suddenly, he threw his head into the mirror and out of sight. When he withdrew his head again, Amy could see his eyes streaming with tears of laughter and a wide grin spread across his face. "Of course, I'm a boy. I have been for over fifty years."

"Are you mocking us?" Amy replied sternly. "Yeah, right, you look about eleven."

He grabbed his sides and began to chuckle. "Eleven? Ha! Twelve in human years, actually! But enough chat for now. I'll see you later, mate."

"Mate?" repeated Jamie, climbing to his knees. "I think you'll find I have already filled the mate position. Now…now…just go and leave us alone."

"Anything you say, Jamie," laughed the boy. "But I'll be back. Now keep the mirror covered. Don't you do anything your Grandad tells you?"

The stranger strode backwards, winked toward Amy and Jamie, and then ran full pelt at the mirror. Like an Olympic swimmer, he dived through the glass and out of the bedroom.

A tiny smile curled the corners of Amy's lips. The Reflection was real! But one obvious question gnawed at her- *if the boy was from The Reflection, why didn't he look like a beast?*

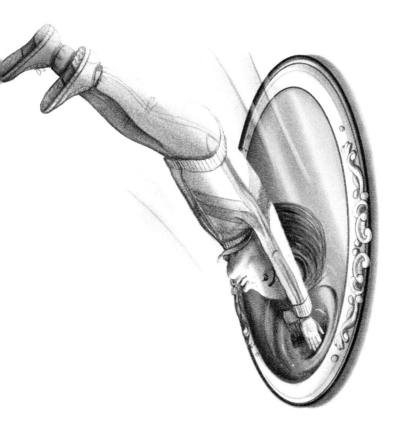

3
Ding Dong

Amy couldn't remember drifting off to sleep. She was just relieved she had woken up unharmed and in her bed. She was also relieved they had used an airbed and didn't sleep tops to tails. Jamie had been moving around so much that he must have thought he was on a bouncy castle. She peeked over a slumbering Jamie to see the towel still on the mirror and the door slightly ajar. *It was all a dream. It had to be.*

A little stone of disappointment plummeted to the bottom of her stomach. But remembering it was Saturday made a little smile dance along her mouth. Staring at the ceiling, she sighed loudly and sank deeper into the mattress. Amy was certainly not a morning person. And judging by Jamie's whistling snore, nor was he. Typically, on weekends, Amy would lie in bed until she had to be physically dragged from it. The temptation of a cooked breakfast, a good show on TV, or even an animal documentary wasn't enough to get her bouncing out of bed. Well, unless it were a brand-new David Attenborough one, then she'd consider it.

"Amy!" came a call from Grandad. "Jamie! Are you up yet?"

She couldn't muster a reply, instead forcing a tiny grunt.

"Get up, you two!"

"Spiderman and three poached eggs, please," replied Jamie groggily.

Amy giggled and wrapped the duvet around herself tighter still.

Grandad could be heard beginning to climb the stairs. Amy knew they still had a few minutes yet. She would have to shift herself only when the second to last stair cried out. She knew that stair too well; it was always skipped when she sneaked downstairs for a midnight feast. Both children grunted and sat up on one elbow as Grandad shuffled into the room.

"Come on, young'uns, best not waste the day in bed." He rested one unsteady knee on the bed and reached over to draw open the curtains. Grandad then wriggled his bottom into the warm bed. "Good to see the towel is still over that mirror, sensible. I'm pleased to see you can be trusted."

Amy and Jamie both gulped.

"Do you know, Grandad, I had the strangest dream last night."

"Me too," added Jamie. "I dreamt that a tiny shiny.."

"Ball flew in through the mirror," suggested Amy.

"Exactly!....Hold on a sec, you mean…" Jamie paused as he caught sight of Grandad.

The old man didn't speak. He didn't even whistle or hum. Instead, his wheezing chest began to quicken. The blood had drained from Grandad's face. He sat stock still and wide-eyed, staring. Amy and Jamie followed his glare.

Now flooding the little box room, the sunlight bounced off all the cuddly animal toys and poured over the walls. But the carpet was most peculiar. It glistened and shimmered like a frosted pavement under a streetlight. *The boy! Reflective dust! It did happen!*

Grandad moved slowly towards the scattering on the floor. "Is that?" he started, poking a finger into the fine dust and swirling it around. "Did you take the towel off the mirror?"

Amy could tell by his tone that this was not the time to confess or even mention the boy. "No, of course not," she lied.

"Are you sure? This is worrying. Very worrying." Grandad began pacing the room.

"I thought it was a fly. Hit it with my shoe during the night."

Grandad licked his lips. "It's an eyerie, or rather it was. Did it see you?"

"An eyerie?" Jamie repeated, in a tone too high pitched to suggest he was an innocent party. "Looks strange."

"Strange possibly, but dangerous, very dangerous. Think of them as little spies. What they see, so can the emperor."

"The emperor? Like the leader of the beasts?" probed Amy.

"That's right. But look, now the eyerie is reflective dust, and I can use this dust!" Grandad replied with a twinkle in his eye. The same twinkle Amy often saw when a yarn was in full flow.

Eyerie, reflective dust, he knows the names, thought Amy. Perhaps everything he said about The Reflection was true.

DING DONG!

Grandad jumped, almost dropping the dust he had delicately brushed into his hand.

BANG!

He pulled his granddaughter tight against his chest and grabbed hold of Jamie's wrist. Amy could feel his heart thumping so hard it shook both their bodies.

BANG! BANG!

"What's their problem?" moaned Amy.

"Yeah, what's their problem?" repeated Jamie. "Don't they know I'm the only one who can bang on your door like that?" He smiled, trying to ease the palpable tension in the room.

"It's them. They're here; too much of a coincidence not to be," whispered Grandad.

A knot in Amy's stomach twisted tight. *Who was at the door?*

DING DONG!

"They've clearly been watching the house. Your mum is at the shop, and they probably think you're at school. They must think I'm alone."

"Who thinks you're alone? Beasts?!" Amy squeaked. "Is it my fault? Because of the eyerie?"

"Goodness no child, it's my fault. It's always been mine. But we can sort this together, Kiddo. Come on, I've got a plan."

Grandad's stories often took Amy on an adventure without leaving the house. But this time, it didn't feel like a story. The hairs on end along her arms told her it was real this time.

4
Lifford

"I'll wait here," offered Jamie, climbing back into bed.

"Both of you stay up here! It's safer. I'll check it out," said Grandad.

"Not without me. I'm going," stated Amy, already opening the door. "And don't even try and stop me."

Grandad tapped his fingers on the handle of his walking stick repeatedly before finally replying. "Okay, but not a word. And you do exactly what I say."

The pair tentatively descended the stairs. Grandad, leading the way, puffed out his chest and fixed his shocking mop of grey hair that stuck out like a toilet brush.

"You'll be fine. Be brave."

The quiver in the old man's voice didn't make Amy feel fine. *Why did she need to be brave?* Surely, if a beast were coming, they wouldn't use the door, and most certainly, they wouldn't ring the bell.

But Grandad walked straight past the front door and into the kitchen.

"Take this," said the old man passing Amy a roll of black bags. "Cover the seats."

Bemused and baffled, she did as directed.

She wasn't quite sure what her grandfather had in mind but with the incessant ringing of the doorbell disturbing the silence in the house, she thought this wasn't the time to ask. She quickly placed a plastic bag over each of the four chairs while Grandad boiled the kettle.

"It's time, my love. Let's do this!"

Amy marched purposefully to the front door, unsure what she wanted more; to face a beast or stop the doorbell from piercing her ears. Grandad followed close behind, his walking stick tapping on the wooden floor quicker than usual. Without even looking through the frosted glass, Amy whipped the door open. She sighed loudly, and her tense body relaxed at seeing a man in uniform.

"About time, child, Detective Inspector White here." The man flashed a police badge.

Amy studied the badge. "You're the police?" she replied, backing away from the bald, pale officer.

"Yes, that's what I said, Detective White," he smiled. His teeth were like a jigsaw puzzle with missing pieces. He hobbled awkwardly towards the girl and her grandad.

Amy tried not to stare as he limped into the house. Looking down at his shoes, it was immediately obvious that one was considerably larger than the other. He was virtually hopping as he followed them into the sitting room.

The detective inspector wiped drool away from the corner of his mouth and tilted his head to survey the room. His wrinkled skin, like the surface of a raisin, sagged to one side. "Hmm, tell me this, where are all your mirrors? Can't see any, strange that. Very strange, I would say."

"Not really," Amy replied with a furrowed brow. "We're starting to paint this week."

"Hmm, convenient that. Well, I think it's peculiar. A home without mirrors isn't a home if you ask me."

Grandad stood statue still and muted. Amy tore her eyes from the policeman to look at the old man. His eyes were as wide as dinner plates, and his short sharp breaths immediately made Amy's heart race.

The police officer used his sleeve and wiped his brow, "Ah, Charlie, I presume. Detective Inspector White." He offered out an enormous shovel of a hand. "It's just a friendly call to ensure that all the human children are safe from dangerous kidnappers."

Human children? Amy instantly clocked his odd remark and took a step away.

Grandad still hadn't moved, and Amy could see his bottom lip tremble. *She thought he was going to cry.*

"I...er...um...," stuttered Grandad, finally taking the officer's hand.

Detective White thrust his hand into Grandad's and violently began shaking it while fixing a deathly stare upon the old man, who was now sweating profusely.

"Tea, Detective?" offered Amy, trying desperately to end the odd exchange.

"Tea? I don't drink tea, Amy," he replied sharply.

"Coffee then," rushed Grandad finally, through panting breaths. "Come on through."

Detective White stumbled forward, leaning on the walls to feel his way. He stopped and stared at a family portrait hanging on the wall for an absurdly long time.

Amy grew more uneasy, shoulders rigid with tension. *How did he know their names? And what was up with that handshake?* She glanced nervously at her grandfather, who forced a smile and winked as he slowly shuffled over to the kettle and cups.

"Do excuse the black bin bags on the chairs," began Grandad. "We'd hate to get paint on the furniture." He spoke without looking at the policeman.

Detective White sat at the table, one foot under the table, the other, large foot, hanging at the side of the chair. His intense staring eyes pierced a hole through the back of Grandad's head the entire time.

Amy neared her quivering grandfather and watched him take the Reflective dust from his pocket.

"You'll take sugar in your coffee, won't you, Detective?" Grandad insisted.

Grandad lifted the dust to his mouth, whispered some words, and sprinkled it into the cup of coffee. A spark lit up his eyes like Christmas fairy lights, and Amy knew instantly that Grandad had a present for the detective. *Was it poison?*

The Detective didn't flinch or reply. He didn't even blink. Instead, he grunted, a deep low grunt that shook his whole body and the table.

Grandad reached for a spoon in the cutlery drawer but was shaking so much it sounded like a baby's rattle. Amy stepped in.

"Let me, Grandad."

The old man rested both hands on the worktop, took a deep breath and nodded.

Amy gave the coffee a frantic stir. "There you go, Detective White," she said, smiling. She placed the red cup down on the kitchen table.

"What are you grinning about, girl?" he snapped. The detective studied the cup before him, then slowly withdrew a hand from his pocket. Using just one solitary finger, he pushed the cup across the table. "How stupid do you think I am?"

Suddenly the detective leapt from his chair, clattering the table and sending half of the cup's contents over the floor. He advanced on Grandad. With his eyes narrowed and his head lowered, he mowed down the old man like a bull would a red flag.

Grandad reached for his walking stick and threw it into the detective's chest. But it had no impact. The salivating police officer continued to hobble forward with purpose.

"Your time has come, Charlie boy. All that aftershave you have on can't mask your fear. You stink of it. It's oozing from every pore. This has been a long time coming!"

A frightful anger suddenly swelled within Amy making her very fingertips tingle. How dare someone threaten her grandad. She clenched her teeth as Detective White snatched hold of Grandad's walking stick, swallowing it almost whole as his enormous hands enveloped the piece of wood. Flashing his rows of crooked teeth, he snapped the stick into tiny pieces and lurched open-mouthed towards Grandad's face.

Grandad furiously swung his arms, searching for anything to help him escape.

The coffee!

In a flash, Amy whizzed around the table, lunged for the cup and, without thought for direction, hurled the remaining contents at the villainous officer, who by now had pinned Grandad's wrists to his sides.

The tussle momentarily stopped as the detective's head snapped around and his gaze fixed upon the girl. Grandad broke free of the policeman's grasp and darted towards his granddaughter.

"What's happening to him?" asked Amy.

"Stand back," replied Grandad, taking her hand. "He's gonna blow!"

The Reflective Dust! What is it? `

By now, Detective White was glowing orange. His eyes were bulging, his lips swollen, and his entire body trembled. He stood up straight, almost levitating, only the toes of his large shoes sweeping the kitchen floor. His body was giving off so much heat that Amy and Grandad had to shield their faces but still couldn't resist peeking through their fingers. Suddenly the detective's body flopped. It completely collapsed in on itself like someone had sucked out his bones. The sagging hissing skin fell onto the tiled floor like wet spaghetti.

Grandad, pinching his nose, took a black bag from a chair and bent down to the simmering mess on the floor, "Now I bet you believe me about those beasts and The Reflection."

At that moment, Jamie peeked through the kitchen door, nose twitching. "I don't know what you're cooking for breakfast, but I'll just have cereal, thanks."

5
Power Pose

When Grandad Charlie finally returned to the kitchen, he wore a clean shirt, equally flamboyant as the previous one. He loved his colourful shirts- swirls, stripes, zig-zags; the more eye-catching, the better. The problem was that staring at one for too long would give you a headache.

Jamie stood motionless, leaning against the sink, his stomach twisting. Slowly he edged his way towards the table and sank into a chair. "Let me get this right," he said. "You're trying to tell me the smell is a dissolved police officer?" He laughed nervously and held back a dry wretch. "I'm so confused."

"Me too," replied Amy. She began frantically spinning a hairband around her wrist. "What happened? How did...who was?" stuttered Amy.

Grandad opened the kitchen window and switched on the kettle. "Tea, anyone?" he asked casually.

"Tea, Grandad? Tea! What on earth just happened?" screeched Amy.

"Ah, okay, but before I begin, I need you both to do something for me. Stand up."

"Ah Grandad, do we have to?"

"Yes, yes, come on. If you want the full story, then stand up and make a power pose." Grandad hauled both children to their wobbly legs.

"A power pose?" asked Jamie.

"It's a pose that makes you feel strong and confident, Jamie. Let me show you."

Grandad folded his fingers behind his head, raised his chin and fixed a steely glare upon the ceiling light.

Amy struck the power pose she'd used many times before with Grandad. She squeezed her hands into a fist and rested a fist on each hip. She stood with her feet shoulder-width apart and looked to her left.

Jamie widened his stance, stretched his arms straight in a wide V, pouted his lips and bobbed his head with arrogance.

"Great job! Perfect! I love it," Grandad grasped. "Now, repeat after me. I am strong!"

"I am strong," the pair repeated unenthusiastically.

"Ah, come on, you can do better than that. Again, I am strong!

"I am strong," they said with a little more conviction.

"I am brave!"

"I am brave!" they announced.

"I am clever!" barked Grandad.

"I am clever!" they repeated.

"I am confident!"

"I am confident!" they both yelled.

"We fear nothing!" screamed Grandad.

"We fear nothing!" Jamie and Amy were twitching with energy and excitement.

"Just brilliant kids, brilliant! I love it. I can feel your strength. And good, because you're going to need it. We are going to need each other. You see, that wasn't a police officer. He was a beast! He's dead now, though, so he won't be doing any more harm."

There was no denying that. The taste of Detective White's disintegrated body still hung in the air.

"And he won't be kidnapping any more children," Grandad added sharply. "But we must be on our guard. No doubt more feeders will be back."

"A feeder? You mean they're eating humans?" asked Amy, fearing she already knew the answer.

Grandad took a good long look at the child before him. "I really shouldn't tell you this. Your Mum will…"

"Never know," interrupted Amy, smiling. "Was Detective White a feeder then? Did you know him?"

"I did, Missy. His real name was Lifford. His only job is to snatch children from their beds at night. Didn't you notice the size of his hands? Feeders have massive hands, helps them scoop up innocent kids. He even tried to snatch me. But I managed to close a door on his foot, snapped the biggest toe off like a twig."

Hands? Thought Amy. She'd seen two people now from The Reflection, and they were both just that, people.

Jamie smacked his dry lips together and asked, "But how did you know he was a beast? Do they all look just like us?"

"Goodness, no!" replied Grandad. "They are revolting creatures. But I had a run-in with Lifford before you see. I'm the reason he has, I mean had, one foot shorter than the other."

DING DONG!

BANG BANG!

Silence fell across the room. All three pairs of eyes jinked nervously at each other.

They couldn't be back already. Could they? Amy's heart raced even faster when it occurred to her they had no reflective dust left and the coffee cup was empty. She bit her bottom lip and put an arm across Jamie to stop him scampering under the table.

"Dad!" came a call through the letterbox in the door. "Amy! I forgot my key!"

A collective sigh filled the kitchen. *Phew!*

"I'll get it," offered Grandad. He stood up, tucked in his shirt, and adjusted his collar.

"We'll get it," Amy said, dragging Jamie towards the front door.

"Ah, thanks, love," started Mum, who then tutted when she saw Amy take the newspaper from her shopping bag and head towards the stairs.

"Eewww, what's that smell?" asked Mum, sniffing the air. "It's disgusting."

"It wasn't me if that's what you are getting at," Grandad remarked, insulted.

"No, this is worse. It smells like someone has died in here."

"Haha, good one," Jamie chuckled nervously, then quick-footed it upstairs.

Amy sat on the end of her bed and read the newspaper aloud slowly:

Tarabally Town Tribune

GIRL ESCAPES SNATCHING!

Police took a giant leap towards retrieving the five missing children in the Spring Rock area, with the revelation that one nine-year-old girl escaped a kidnap attempt.

At approximately 1 am, young Tracey Yan fought off a perpetrator in her bedroom.

Police have warned that the culprits are dangerously focussed on their mission and all people, children and adults alike, should be on guard twenty-four-seven.

Police stated that young Tracey is extremely shaken up and traumatised by the incident, babbling that an animal inside her mirror tried to take her. Experts assert that Tracey has reverted to a state of fantasy to cope with the situation because she is frightened beyond the ability of rational thought.

Parents, guardians, grandparents and residents of the area are all asked to be extra vigilant. Before putting your children to bed, please ensure your house is secure, all windows, doors and possible entry points are fastened shut, and lock your children in their rooms.

Just as Amy finished, she heard Grandad wheezing as he reached the noisy second-to-last stair. She folded the paper and followed the old man to his room, Jamie in tow.

Their eyes darted around the room as they entered, both heads bobbing like figures on the dash of a car. *As expected, there was not a mirror in sight.*

"Did you two lose something?"

Amy shook her head. "No, look, it's the beasts, Grandad." She handed him the paper.

"Reading glasses are downstairs. What's it say?"

"A child escaped. But the police, they're making things worse! The only advice is to lock your children in their bedrooms," gulped Amy. "There's nowhere to run then. We need to tell them."

"You want me to tell the police that beasts inside the mirrors are to blame for the kidnappings? They'll never believe me. They'll think I've lost my marbles. And they won't be too pleased when I say it's all my fault."

"What do you mean?" asked Jamie.

"It's me they're after. It always has been. Wanting their revenge." Grandad's ears were pricked, listening for Mum.

"I never thought they would actually catch up with me, though. But this current Emperor, he's different. He won't give up. Even after almost fifty years. He would have sent Lifford."

Amy sat at the foot of the bed, twisting the hairband around her fingers. "What do you mean, current Emperor? What happened to the old one? Did you…..kill him?" she added with a gulp.

The old man stared Amy in the eye and nodded.

"You killed their leader?" screeched Amy.

"I did. I had to. That reflective dust is powerful stuff! It just needs a command."

"Really?" said Jamie, in a high-pitched tone, a little too loud for a secret conversation and a little too high-pitched for an eleven-year-old boy. He blushed. But wide-eyed, he was hooked, utterly spellbound. Grandad was undeniably truthful, speaking without a smile or a smirk.

Amy had missed moments like this when she believed every word of her grandfather's story. She was so proud and even more pleased that Jamie was present to witness it all.

"How do you know so much about The Reflection, Grandad?" quizzed the intrigued girl.

"I've never been, if that's what you are trying to say, ridiculous thought. Sure, how could I? Why would I?" He lost eye contact with the eager children and reached for a drink of water on the sideboard.

"No, I'm not saying that. I just wondered how you know about the beasts."

"Ah well, that's easy. After Lifford and killing the Emperor Beast, I made friends with a third beast, Crumlish. He told me everything, including how to make the poison from reflective dust."

"Well, that's it then!" announced Amy. "We need to make more poison. Because if the police can't help, we must do something."

Grandad released a hearty laugh that shook the whole bed. "If only, sweetheart. But I'm too slow and too old. And anyway, we don't have any Reflective dust."

Amy looked at Jamie and smiled but said nothing.

6
Ready?

The house was silent, save for Grandad's snoring and a hissing radiator on the landing. Amy sat in her room alone, contemplating her next move. Without Jamie present, she didn't feel quite so brave. She leapt to her feet and shook herself. *Come on, you can do this!* She marched purposefully towards the mirror, only to abruptly stop when she was in touching distance. She flicked her tongue pensively between her top and bottom lip. She paused, took a deep breath and began slowly pacing her room, treading between rubbish, clothes and books on the floor; all the while never taking her narrowed eyes from the mirror.

Would removing the towel even work? Would eyeries fly in again? Might the boy return too?

Amy struck her power pose and whispered, "Have no fear." Her pace quickened and she ventured towards the mirror. She reached for the corner of the towel still covering the reflective glass. Tentatively she revealed a few little inches, took a step back and waited.

Nothing. No eyeries. No boy.

Undeterred, she strode towards the mirror again, pulling the towel further down.

Then she backed away and perched on the edge of her bed. Amy's tapping feet were knocking so ferociously that they were heating up. They still didn't tap as fast as a woodpecker; they can hit wood over twenty times a second. She dared not blink. Her enormous, blue eyes remained fixated on the bit of mirror revealed.

Amy's sweaty hands fidgeted endlessly as her mind raced like a greyhound from the traps. *If the Emperor wanted revenge as badly as Grandad claimed, where were the eyeries?* She rose to her feet, slid over to the mirror and whipped off the towel completely. No sooner had it hit the floor when the boy dived into the room headfirst. He rolled into a tumble and expertly landed on his feet like a gymnast. In the same motion, he bounced back towards the mirror and concealed it again behind the towel. If Amy could catch her breath, she might have awarded ten points.

"You're playing a dangerous game, young lady. Weren't you told to keep the mirror covered?" The boy pulled his dark joggers, that had ridden up, back down towards his ankles and adjusted his twisted grey sweat jumper into position.

"All right, Grandpa," Amy snorted as she threw the duvet on the bed.

"It's CD, actually," the stranger answered, his cheeks glowing crimson.

"CD? Is that your name?"

"Yeah, got a problem?" he retorted while shaping the middle parting in his hair.

"No, not at all," she took a deep breath and flopped onto her bed releasing a long obvious sigh.

"What's wrong with you?" CD asked with a tone of concern.

"Oh, nothing. You couldn't do it anyway," Amy replied, feigning interest.

"Couldn't do what?" he retorted.

"Take me into The Reflection." *If the eyeries won't come to me, I'll go to them!*

"You're very trusting, too trusting. You need to be more careful. How do you know I'm not here to kidnap you? And you're asking me to take you in."

Amy stared at the human boy before her. Did grotesque savage beasts even exist?

"Well, if you wanted to snatch me, I guess you would have done it by now."

"Too true." CD began to lunge and stretch. "Right then, let's go."

"Really?" squeaked Amy, standing up spritely and brushing herself down. *Well, that was easy.*

"Yeah, go on then," CD began. "Want to see your bedroom in The Reflection? It couldn't be much worse than this pigsty," he added, looking around.

Amy snarled at the insult and defiantly agreed, "Come on then."

"The mirror is open since I've just come through. Just pop your head in."

Amy stood at the edge of her bed in a navy onesie with a sudden intense warm tingling in her body. "I still don't see how this will work," she said.

"Of course, it will. Imagine the mirror is a portal, and I've opened it. Look-" CD pulled the towel back like a curtain, ducked his head inside, and effortlessly pulled his head back out. "Brrr, it's a cold one in there. See, easy!"

Dry-mouthed and wide-eyed, Amy made a beeline for the mirror. This was it, the first step on a mission to create more poison and rescue the missing children. She stared straight ahead, pushed her sleeves up, stretched out a hand and moved it towards the mirror slowly.

"Wow! What are you doing? Not your hand, you want a look, don't you? Your head! Stick your head in. It's safe, I promise," CD smiled.

Amy did just as CD had done. She tentatively pulled the towel to one side to reveal the shiny glass, then took a deep breath.

"Do it quickly, get it over and done with, like pulling off a plaster," CD smirked.

As directed, the eager girl thrust her head straight into the mirror. SMACK!

She let out a single solitary scream. "Ouch!"

CD was bent over double laughing.

"What's that all about?" Amy snapped, rubbing her forehead.

"I can't believe you fell for that. No human can get into The Reflection without a beast's touch. You mean your Grandad Charlie didn't tell you that? Ah, so perhaps he doesn't know everything after all."

Amy's brow was so furrowed that her eyes could barely be seen.

"Relax, it was only a joke."

"Does it look like I'm laughing?" she snapped.

"Okay, okay, I'm sorry," CD said in a tone that suggested he wasn't at all. "You're brave, Amy. I'll give you that." He fixed the towel securely over the mirror. "But you wouldn't be if you knew what awaits a human in there."

"Ah it's okay. I knew you couldn't take me. You're scared. I can see that. It's fine, I understand," she murmured, her head throbbing.

"You'd be scared too if you knew what they'd do to you," CD argued. "You in The Reflection, ha! You'd last as long as a pork chop in a pool of piranhas."

"I'd be fine. I'd manage," she sniffed. "I've got my ways to survive."

"You mean your abilities."

Amy could feel herself stop breathing. Her heart rate quickened as she shuffled her feet and looked at the floor.

"Relax, use one of your breathing exercises. I'll not be telling anyone. That includes your grandfather," he smirked. "Anyway, super strength or invisibility won't help you much," retorted CD. "You're not ready for what's in there."

"I was born ready."

"Ready? Where did I get Amy from? Why does everyone call you Amy," CD enquired, wearing a confused look on his face.

"No, it's...look, never mind," drawled Amy, rolling her eyes.

"Ready or Amy, you wouldn't last a minute in there without me,"

"Really? Prove it then!"

"I will then!" CD marched towards the girl, snatched her hand and hauled her towards the mirror.

7
Into the Reflection

Clinging on to Amy's quivering hand, CD climbed into the mirror and out of sight. Slowly her arm disappeared. Wincing, she resisted, tugging back towards the safety of her bedroom. But CD was strong, and despite regretting her decision, Amy's body was beginning to slide into The Reflection. The moment she could no longer see any of her limbs, she felt a sudden flash of fear tingle every muscle in her arm. She abruptly pulled back with such velocity that CD shot back into the bedroom like a catapult.

"What's wrong?" asked CD, climbing to his feet. "Scared? I knew it."

"No!" insisted Amy, with a forced snarl. "It's just that it's wet. I didn't expect it."

"It's not. It's just cold. You'll get used to it."

Amy took a deep breath and offered out her hand. "Okay. Let's do this!"

Linked together, they ventured into the mirror. It parted like a still reflective pond. As Amy stepped into the mirror, her stomach lurched forward, springing a butterfly to life in her belly. But not any ordinary butterfly; it was a Queen Alexandra Birdwing butterfly. The biggest in the world, nearly 30 centimetres in width, and it was flapping in a panic inside her stomach.

She began humming to herself as she was sucked into The Reflection, leaving her bedroom behind. As quickly as it started, it was over. And they were standing in what looked like her room. It was identical; the same bed, posters, furniture, and even the overflowing bin were in the same corner of the room. There was only one protruding noticeable difference; the floor was covered in grey dust, and the colours were faded- the carpet, the wallpaper, the bed sheets, everything was dull, lifeless. Even a weed was growing into the room through a crack in the wall, and the streetlight outside that normally broke in through a gap in the blinds was extinguished. Most chilling was that a thin layer of frosted ice covered the window, concealing the outside world and hiding the beasts that lurked.

Amy released CD's grip and walked towards her collection of fluffy animal toys. She blew on them and sent a cloud of dirt into the air. It hung motionless. Then she noticed the lack of sound. There was no washing machine rumbling, no hum of electricity or heating in the house, no passing cars or rustling trees. It wasn't a place she wanted to stay for long. And yet she needed to. She had to get more Reflective dust.

"Right, you've had a look. Now, let's go!" CD started moving towards the mirror on the back of the door. It was a perfect window into Amy's colourful, yet messy, real room.

"Just a few more minutes. I want to see more."

"No, no, not wise, come on." CD was frantically shaking his head.

"Ah, please, I can't do it without you. I need your help." It wasn't really a lie. She'd seen CD crush eyeries before, and obviously, he knew more about The Reflection than she did.

He sighed and stepped aside to reveal the bedroom door. Amy reached out for the handle to find it was on the opposite side. It hadn't occurred to her that they were inside a reflection after all. A glance around at her posters and the writing confirmed her hunch. Everything was in reverse.

The metal knob on the door was so cold to touch that it was painful. But it was an even stranger sensation to swing the door open to the left instead of the right.

Every breath expelled shot out like someone who was puffing on a cigar. Amy's onesie and slippers were offering little warmth. She was relieved that the current bubble of fear sparked an ability to resist the cold like a Red Flat Bark Beetle, which, with protein in its cells, can survive the coldest climates.

Amy wasn't made to feel any warmer when she tentatively descended the stairs. Each of the fourteen stairs, with their frozen wooden panels, creaked and moaned with every footstep.

When surveying the hall and sitting room, Amy noticed all the mirrors were back on the walls. But there was no window into the real world, no reflection. Instead, each was black and lifeless, like a switched-off television.

"So that's why Grandad took our mirrors down and covered them," she whispered to herself.

Trying to frantically comprehend and survey all the sights before her was a stressful task, particularly with the threat of a beast nearby. But why was The Reflection world so tidy? Newspapers were folded on the coffee table, coats hung on their pegs next to the front door, and even shoes were neatly in pairs at the foot of the stairs. Amy had imagined things flying around in The Reflection world. If a car moved in the real world, it would surely move in The Reflection too. But it seemed every item had a home. A place it should be, just as in her world. Growing in confidence and her heart rate slowing down, she darted to the drawer under the television. There, wrapped tightly in a ball, was the phone charger; in the place Mum always put it, and not in the wall where it usually was left. Amy then raced to the window and scratched a little patch clear of frost and peeked outside. The street was eerily dark, but the intrepid girl could still see that every neighbour's car was parked in their driveway.

"Now we need to go," rushed CD. "This is too dangerous for both of us!"

But Amy was already unlocking the front door.

"Are you crazy? What are you playing at?" CD wedged his foot against the door.

But it was too late.

Four eyeries slipped in through the gap. Maybe it was six, ten, perhaps. They were moving so fast Amy couldn't keep count. They shot in like tiny shiny bullets, screaming as they ripped the air in two. CD began using his hand like a tennis racket and swatted a few against the wall. **SPLAT!**

Amy had once seen a movie where an old Chinese sensei caught a fly with chopsticks, and she now knew how he must have felt. Between her thumb and index finger quivered a shiny little ball. She watched it intensely, then slowly began to squeeze. With ease, it popped open like a crushed grape.

The dim glow from the ceiling light bounced off the dust as it trickled towards the ground. Soon the floor was filled with a scattering of mesmerising reflective dust.

CD slammed the door closed. "Do you know what you just did?" he started. "What are you doing now?

"What does it look like?" Amy replied sarcastically. "Getting the dust. Well, don't just stand there!" She began shoving it by the handful into her pockets.

"And what are you going to do with that?"

"Something you should be doing. I'll get my Grandad to make more poison. Then we'll go and rescue those kidnapped," she said, waving a fist full of dust.

CD began to laugh, too loud and too forced to be genuine. Then he abruptly stopped and glanced around. "You can't use reflective dust!" he whispered.

"Want to bet," replied Amy. "My Grandad has already used some; on Lifford."

"Lifford? The feeder?" asked CD, his eyes now wider than before. He stared at the red-haired girl before him. "Where did you hear that name?"

"He came to my house; big mistake. He's dead now."

"He's dead?" repeated CD, "How?"

"My Grandad used this Reflective dust on him," said Amy, climbing back to her feet.

"Ha! Impossible!" he snorted. "It can't be done, no way; you must be wrong."

"Look, you can check our bin if you want. Lifford's disintegrated body is in a black bag. Just stop arguing and get the rest of the dust. My pockets are full."

CD smiled and bent down, "Well, Lifford certainly won't be missed. But you're mistaken again. Not all of his body is in that bag. There's a human somewhere with part of old Lifford's missing toe."

8
Cold Shower

"Mum, where's Grandad?"

Amy's Mum stood at the top of a ladder, drill in hand, tool belt around her waist and protective goggles over her eyes, "He was in the shower, Sweetie. Should be finished by now, I'd say."

Had it not been for the reflective dust tingling in her pockets, Amy would have believed last night's adventure was a dream.

She bounded back upstairs in search of the old man. There wasn't a moment to waste. The arrival of another beast was surely inevitable. They needed to prepare, and they needed poison.

Grandad showered every morning, scrubbing himself red raw and layered up with deodorant and aftershave. He'd spend an age in there. It did little to mask his old man smell though, and it caused many an argument. It was partly why Mum was trying to convert the downstairs loo.

"Mum! He's not in the shower." Amy hollered over the hum of the drill. "Mum!"

"Check his room then. He's up there somewhere. Do I have to do everything for you?"

Amy raced from room to room, but they were all empty. Where was he? Amy held her breath and tried to listen over the racket downstairs. There was nothing.

Grandad's room was perfectly tidy. The bed sheets, as always, were pulled ridiculously tight and tucked under the mattress, creating a surface so hard it could be built upon. Amy sat on the cold hard bed and felt her heart pound against her rib cage. She traced her dry tongue along her lips. *There was no way a beast could have taken him, was there?*

Amy carefully withdrew the reflective dust from her pockets and poured it into an empty water bottle on Grandad's dresser.

"Amy!" called Mum. "Get a move on!"

Upon hearing Mum climb from the ladder, Amy lifted the bottle and headed downstairs.

"I told you he wasn't up there."

"Watch it, young lady," snapped Mum. "Now go and get your breakfast."

"Sorry, Mum, it's just that...."

"Good morning, all," chirped Grandad, descending the stairs. "Now, who fancies some bacon sandwiches before school?"

"Where were you?" asked Amy, grabbing his hand. "Oh you're freezing."

"That's that....err..it's that shower, the water turned cold, blasted thing."

"I checked the bathroom," she replied. "And the bedrooms. You weren't upstairs at all."

"Ah, Ams, relax. They'd never get me." He winked. "Now, breakfast, brown or red sauce?"

Grandad was lying. Wasn't he? Amy took a deep breath and gulped. This was her beloved Grandfather; her heart stung a little at the thought. Her mind was swimming with questions. Why was CD so adamant that Grandad couldn't use the reflective dust? She moved to follow the old man towards the kitchen and find, not if for certain if he could make more poison.

"I don't think so, Missy," began Mum. "You're already late. I'll drive you to school. Dad, she'll have a sandwich to go."

9
Prying Eyes

"Are you nuts?! I mean, have you completely lost it?" Jamie was pacing around Amy as she sat at her school desk. "You see, this is the sort of stuff you need me around for. Someone has got to stop you from doing idiotic things. Think of what could have happened. You're lucky to still be here. That boy could have left you there, or worse! Then where would I be, hey? I bet you didn't consider me during all of this." He finally sat down next to her, collapsing into his seat. He threw his head back and sighed towards the sky.

"I did, actually. I thought of how you'd love it. It was like one of those multiverses from those comics you love."

Jamie suddenly sat up to attention. "Go on…"

Amy threw open her school bag and placed it under Jamie's chin. "See!"

"Reflective dust, I assume. I knew you were up to something; you had that look in your eye. It's poisonous, isn't it?"

"It will be once my Grandad turns it into poison."

"Well then, let's get to him," urged Jamie.

"That's my plan, but he doesn't need to hear the whole story. Let's not bore him with details of how I came to have the dust," smiled Amy.

Unfortunately, the school day dragged by painfully slowly. Not helped by the fact that Amy peeked in her bag every five minutes to stare at the shimmering bottle. Lessons had been replaced with constant lectures about stranger danger and how to signal for help. Mrs Gallen stressed how safe the children are in school and once at home with locked doors, nothing could happen to them. A twisting knot was squeezed tighter and tighter in the pit of Amy's stomach as she fought back the urge to tell them just how wrong they were. But like Grandad said, who on earth would believe her?

At 3pm, hundreds of parents, grandparents and childminders gathered outside the school- pushing and squeezing their way towards the front. To any unknowing by-passer, it looked more like a rock concert, with the main act being somewhere in the direction of the rusty green gates.

People weren't too quick in dispersing either. The arrival of every child was greeted with celebration and an extra-long hug. Missing children, worry and stress understandably had a strange effect on people.

To Amy's surprise and joy, Grandad stood at the gates. The old man never did the school runs. Mainly because they'd have to leave at 7am to reach school on time. Grandad moved frustratingly slowly, hindered further by his insistence to speak to everyone he passed.

"Where's Mum?" asked Amy.

"What, I'm not good enough?" Grandad replied sarcastically. "She's stuck up a ladder again," he smiled.

"I know the feeling," injected Jamie. "I was once stuck up a slide. It must have been two storeys high. I was only four years old though, so understandable."

"Ahh, it was five little steps up to that slide, Jamie. And it was only last week." Amy giggled.

Jamie blushed and scratched his head. "That's enough about me. Didn't you want to show your Grandad something?"

"Oh, sounds intriguing," replied Grandad, leaning on his walking stick and turning to face the children.

"Grandad, I heard there were three more kids taken last night. I think it's time we made some poison," she said, unzipping her bag.

"Shhhh, put that away! Not here," rushed Grandad. Twitching nervously, he forced the bottle back into Amy's bag. "Too many prying eyes and sensitive ears." With one hand he clutched his lower back and quickened his pace. The rubber on the sole of his new walking stick silently led the way as the muted trio made for home at a record pace.

Amy was first to dart towards the kitchen, squeezing through the doorframe just ahead of Jamie, who made a beeline for the fridge. She withdrew the bottle from her bag and delicately centred it on the kitchen table with such care and delicacy that you'd be forgiven for thinking it was a priceless artefact.

The mop of grey hair seemed to stand on end a little further as the old man staggered into the kitchen and stared at the dust like a mother might her newborn child. He then quickly pushed closed the kitchen door.

"How on earth?" he asked, in a tone that pressed upon Amy that he wasn't impressed.

"Well, she didn't go into The Reflection and get it herself, if that's what you're suggesting," stated Jamie.

Amy shot a steely glare at her oblivious friend, who had resumed making his sandwich.

"Of course not. That's impossible. She can't pass through to The Reflection. Almost nobody can. So, how did you come by this then?" Grandad asked, leaning in and tilting his good left ear towards his granddaughter.

"They were in my room last night, Grandad. Buzzing around, just like the previous ones, they woke me up."

"They? Was there more than one? They didn't see anything did they?" His fingers frantically tapped the table while his eyes studied the bottle's contents. "You see, the Emperor sees what an eyerie does; it's why he sends them out."

"No, they didn't get a chance. I threw my blanket over them like a net and stomped all over them."

"How, though? You didn't take the cover off the mirror, did you?"

"Of course not," she lied. "I'm not stupid."

"It's my fault then. I must have missed a mirror somewhere," he said, looking to the ceiling in thought. "Just like it's my fault they've taken more children. Killing Lifford has only bought us time. Look here, Amy," he said. He lifted a newspaper from the worktop and spread it across the table. "Today's appeal shows all the missing children and the dates they were taken."

The girl studied the map printed in the newspaper. It even had the children numbered in the order they were taken.

"Look at that pattern," Grandad gasped; a lump in his throat stopped him mid-sentence. "They're getting closer with each kidnapping. Closer to me."

"Closer to our house," added Amy. A chill crept down her spine.

"Do you think they've been getting information from the kids," remarked Jamie. "You know, to get to you."

"I'm afraid you might be right, young man," Grandad replied sorrowfully. "It was only a matter of time before their interrogations eventually led to a Grandad Charlie."

"So, you think the missing kids could still be alive?" Amy asked brightly.

"I'd assume so. They wouldn't get much information from them otherwise."

"Well, what are we waiting for? Make more poison and let's rescue them." Amy bounced on the spot, from one foot to the other, while tossing the bottle in her hand.

"No need, Sweetheart. The Reflectionists will sort it."

"The who?" probed the girl.

"Just stop worrying. It will all be sorted," began Grandad. "Of course, I'd love to do something. I would. But I'm too old and too frail."

"We'll do it then," stated Amy.

"We will?" asked Jamie incredulously.

"Sure, all we need is a beast's touch to get into The Reflection."

"What did you say?" quizzed Grandad. "What was that about a beast's touch?"

Flustered, she quickly interrupted, "Come on, it's obvious, isn't it? Otherwise, we'd fall into The Reflection anytime we touched a mirror."

Grandad snatched the bottle and stared at the girl suspiciously. He bit his bottom lip pensively before finally replying, "You're a bright one, Kiddo. And I suppose you're right. Best we make poison, only to protect ourselves though. You're going nowhere, I'm afraid."

"Ah well, if you insist. I was so looking forward to going too," added Jamie, trying to suppress a smile.

10
The Command

Grandad darted around the kitchen like a goldfish in its bowl, searching every cupboard, drawer and shelf. Amy was convinced he must have been possessed when she heard him chanting and muttering to himself repeatedly.

"Don't just stand there gawping, kids. Go and fetch me the deodorants upstairs," he said eagerly. "Check your Mum and Dad's room too. Get me any perfumes and aftershaves."

"They'll go nuts, Grandad."

"It'll be fine. They'll understand," he said as he withdrew a huge pot from below the sink.

They'll understand? Do they know about the beasts and poison too? Amy's train of thought was interrupted by Grandad's enthusiasm. It was infectious and exciting.

"Why all the smellies?" asked Jamie, entering the kitchen, clinking the perfume bottles he cradled in his arms.

"It's to cover the smell of fear," replied Amy.

The old man affixed an admiring gaze upon his granddaughter. "Nothing gets past you, my love."

"It was something that Lifford said before we dealt with him," she smiled.

"You're right. A beast loves the smell of fear, especially in a child. It drives them wild with hunger. They can smell it from miles away."

"Like an elephant can smell water from three miles away."

"I suppose, so if we want to get close enough to hit them with poison, then we need to mask the smell. In fact, douse yourself with some and keep it handy," said Grandad.

"What's the racket about?" yelled Mum, temporarily stopping drilling. "Make sure you tidy any mess you make in there!"

Now resembling a witch's cave, the kitchen smelled like the fragrance department in a shopping centre. Grandad placed a 'cauldron' on the cooker.

"What now?" Amy asked eagerly.

"Now we bung everything together, then just add the reflective dust. This'll do the job on them. No doubt about it."

Together the trio frantically began emptying bottles, spraying aerosols and pouring in washing powder.

"Where's the dust?" asked Jamie, searching through the empty bottles on the kitchen table.

"It's here." Grandad leaned his walking stick against the table, withdrew the bottle from his back pocket and began to unscrew the cap. "I'll command it to kill any evil beasts it comes in contact with."

"Command it?" enquired Amy. "What do you mean command it?"

"Just a few words. I told you, I know all about these beasts in The Reflection. Think of it as...as...a spell." He smiled and winked at the two children.

"I've got it all up here," the sweaty man replied, pointing to his head.

"What is it?" asked Amy, moving closer and pulling Jamie with her. "In case we need to make poison sometime."

"I can't tell you, not yet. You're not ready."

"I'm ready!" she insisted, standing on her tiptoes to meet her grandfather's eyes.

"Not yet, Princess. But soon."

Grrr. Princess! Again! What is it with adults thinking they know best? When you're old enough, when you're ready, when you're more mature. If Grandad only knew what she had already done and what she was about to do with the poisonous spray. Amy knew there was no point pressing him, though, especially while his eyes were narrow and he spoke with clipped tones.

Grandad began muttering again. While watching anxiously, Amy held her breath and listened very carefully to hear the command.

A little smile danced playfully along Grandad's lips as he started;

"Dust from the Reflection, past Emperors are thee,

Heed my words and listen to me.

I am your master, I command you to kill.

Evil beasts from the Reflection, you can do it at will.

A hit from you and the beast shall breathe no more,

Burn away, melt, damn them to the core."

Grandad was jittery with excitement. He began stirring the liquids in the pot with a ladle. The mixture spun around violently. Like a moth to a flame, Amy and Jamie were sucked in. A conveyor belt of eye-stinging aroma was expelled. An inhaled lungful burned their insides. But there was a darkness in the light mixture, black clouds forming in the eye of the tornado. It reminded Amy that this was a deadly weapon.

"So where are we going to keep the poison?" asked the intrigued girl, wide-eyed and eager to get possession of the mixture.

Grandad, without thinking, said, "Grab me a water gun from the shed."

"I don't use water guns anymore," snorted Amy, blushing in front of Jamie.

"I do," interjected Jamie. "Want me to go to my house and get one?"

"No need, lad. Amy, grab me another, quickly!"

"Another?" she asked.

"Yeah," replied Grandad. "I'll explain later. But first, I need that water gun."

Amy took off like a shot out the back door and down to the shed at the end of the garden. *What a weapon this could be!* She could remember owning a huge water pistol with two barrels and a pump action. That could hit a beast from twenty metres away.

However, her search proved fruitless. She slumped back into the kitchen with a glum expression.

"Well," pressed Grandad.

"This is it," she said, handing over a pitiful handheld green water gun. "Where are they all? I used to have a box full."

"Must have used them all," muttered Grandad.

"What do you mean?" interrupted Jamie. "So, do you need mine?"

"Look, that'll do fine for now. It's just to protect you."

Grandad pulled the little plug on the base of the gun's handle and carefully poured some of the mixture in. Amy watched as the dirty yellow mixture filled the plastic gun. When she was handed it, she put it to her ear. It sounded alive, like champagne bottles popping.

"What are you doing with the rest, Grandad?"

"Back up, my darling. You just never know."

He raced to the fridge and rummaged in the bottom sweet and biscuit drawer. "Damn!" He barked.

"What's wrong?" pressed Amy.

"Drawers practically empty. I need sweets. Or something I can inject the leftover mixture into."

"Will this work?" asked Jamie, offering him a packet of Maltesers, not before he popped a final one into his mouth.

"Ahh, those are perfect!" Grandad patted the boy on the back and then spooned the remaining mixture into a syringe from the medicine cupboard. Then he injected the poison into the chocolate balls. "Delicious deadly bullets."

"I heard your command," beamed Amy.

"Yeah, me too," smiled Jamie.

"But can you remember it?" smirked Grandad. "Like all of it. It has to be said in a particular way, a special way. Only a few of us can do it."

Amy didn't reply.

"Ah, don't worry; plenty of time yet. And just think, you'll be the third family member who knows the commands."

"The third?" Amy enquired.

Grandad either ignored her question or didn't hear her as he began clearing the kitchen. "Now, don't breathe a word of this to anyone."

Amy nodded in agreement as she threw an elbow at Jamie. He nodded too.

"I'm confused about the Reflective dust," Jamie said with great interest. "How exactly do you know the command for it?"

"I've already told you. Crumlish, the friendly beast, told me how to do it. That's how I had poison to kill Emperor Dungloe when he came for me. Such a shame Crumlish was snatched. He could have taught me so much more."

"Snatched? Is he dead?" squeaked Jamie.

"I'd assume so. I don't think any emperor would take kindly to a beast helping a human, especially one that had killed the previous Emperor."

"Hold on a second. You had told us that Crumlish arrived *after* Emperor Dungloe and Lifford. You said he was the third beast you had met," Amy stated.

"That's right, he arrived last," Grandad replied sharply.

"How did you know how to make the poison then?"

"Well...well...well," Grandad stuttered. "It was a long time ago; I'm becoming a little confused in my old age. He must have arrived before. Now I think about it; it was definitely before."

Amy bit her bottom lip. Grandad was never confused. He just rhymed off a command decades old. What was he hiding? The little seed of doubt planted in the forest of her mind was already growing.

11
But

Amy lay wide-eyed on top of her bed, with one hand cupping the water pistol filled with poison below her pillow and the other clenched in a fist; still fuming that Jamie couldn't stay overnight. What did she expect though on a school night?

Despite promising Jamie that she'd wait before trying to return to The Reflection, she just didn't have time. Nobody did. The moment Grandad's snoring shattered the silence in the house, she would whip that cover off the mirror and ready herself for the return of CD. She wouldn't have to wait long. Grandad could nod off walking, so tucked up in his bed posed no problems.

Determined and now prepared, Amy gripped the pistol in her right hand, finger poised over the trigger, and in the other hand, she held a tennis racket found in the shed earlier, just in case any eyeries swooped in. She marched towards the door and with one sweeping move, revealed the full-length mirror.

No eyeries arrived. No CD. No beast, either.

They wouldn't give up. Not when they were so close. Would they?

Amy left the towel on the ground and climbed back into bed. She brushed her red hair behind her ears and stared unblinkingly at the mirror. The hours dragged by. By the time she had fallen into an uneasy sleep, the sunlight was already breaking in through the blinds.

"School, Amy! Get up!" came a holler from Mum.

This was not the time for school. Armed with poison, this was the time for a rescue mission in The Reflection. There was only one logical solution.

Amy leapt from her bed and began frantically completing star jumps in the centre of her room. Once sufficiently hot enough, she took the glass of water on her bedside cabinet and poured some into her hands. She dabbed her forehead, splashed a little on the back of her neck and then shook her hands dry. Wrapping her arms around her tummy, she staggered out onto the landing. She mustered up a whimpering cough and waited for someone to dupe.

Grandad was first to appear, hobbling from his room, already fully dressed and smelling like mint and shoe polish.

"You're not looking too well, young lady."

"Not well, Grandad. Tummy. Need to stay at home," Amy groaned.

Mum then came from the bathroom, a towel around her hair.

Grandad felt his granddaughter's forehead and tapped her cheeks. "Reckon you're coming down with something. Probably best she stays in bed today, Maggie."

Mum threw a look at Amy like a double-edged sword, one of disappointment and annoyance.

"Hmmm, I don't think so, Dad. Amy's fine, I'm sure of it. Go on and get dressed for me, Sweetie. We'll talk about this later," said Mum, escorting a resigned Amy into her room.

"Sick? Amy, really?" whispered Mum. "Weren't you asked to keep your abilities hidden around Grandad? You can't get sick, remember!"

"Exactly, so being sick is completely normal. Throws him off the scent."

Mum paused and silently stared at her daughter, who grinned back.

"Sometimes, young lady, you are too smart for your own good." Mum tried to remain stern, but Amy could see her eyes smile.

"Soooo," enquired Amy.

"Soooo," repeated Mum, "You're still going to school. Now get ready." She gently closed Amy's bedroom door behind her.

"She's not ill, Dad."

"Sure, the poor child is sweating, maybe even a fever," said Grandad. "Let her stay at home with me."

"All faked, and I wonder who taught her those little stunts. Trust me, Dad; she's completely fine. Just tired. Her eyes are hanging out of her head. That'll be you and your stories."

Amy's ear was pressed hard against the door listening to the exchange.

"I want no more talk of beasts, mirrors, and nonsense around her again," continued Mum. "This is not the time."

"But.." began Grandad.

"Look, I know you think you're distracting her, entertaining her even. But I don't think it's helping. She's still only a child, Dad."

"Maybe, but an amazing child, she would make a wonderful Reflectionist someday."

"You're not talking to an eleven-year-old now, Dad. Let it go. I don't need your stories. She's going to school, end of. Eight children are missing now. Eight! It's best we keep things as normal as possible."

"You're right, my love; of course you are. She'd be safer there, indeed. They'd never risk revealing themselves in public. The cowards only move under the cover of night."

Mum sighed loudly and stormed off.

Safer in school? Grandad was not letting this go. *Why didn't he just come clean and confess all to Mum? And what's a Reflectionist?* The lack of action made the girl only more eager to investigate The Reflection. But first, she needed CD, and if he wasn't prepared to appear in her bedroom, then at least the school had plenty of mirrors too.

Barrack Street Primary School was your typical school, filled with teachers, pupils, colourful walls, rules and huge dinner queues every Friday. Mmm chips! The children were unfortunately not so aesthetically pleasing in their brown uniforms. They had the misfortune of looking like they were out of date chocolate bars.

At the school gates, every parent held their child tighter for a little longer. Amy broke free from Mum's grasp just as she tried to land a kiss on her forehead. She turned around just long enough to see Mum drawn in by the gaggle of parents outside the gates, all heavy-eyed with faces awash with woes.

"Look, Amy," whispered Jamie, holding open his bag as she entered the classroom. "It's my brother's old mobile phone."

Amy's stomach fluttered and a little eek escaped from her throat.

She wasn't allowed a mobile phone until she was officially a teenager. This was a monumental moment. Jamie having a mobile, felt like she had one too.

"Oh, what's that?" sniggered Conor Phillips. "Looks like a brick! How old is that thing?" The blonde-haired boy moved to lean over Amy and throw a hand into Jamie's bag.

Amy felt a frightful burning sensation tingle through her body and flash towards her very fingertips. With one hand, and without leaving her seat, she pushed Conor's chest, sending him stumbling back towards his cronies. Super strength was nothing new. She recalled the list of animal DNA coursing in her blood and knew instantly it was a leafcutter ant. That tiny insect can carry up to fifty times its body weight.

"Deep breaths, Amy. He's not worth it." Jamie left his mobile in his bag and began demonstrating finger breathing with his friend. "Come on, do it with me."

Together they raced the index finger of their right hand along the length of the left thumb, breathing in at the same time. At the tip of the thumb, they paused and held their breath. Then they breathed out as they moved down the thumb. Breathing in, then moved up along the left index finger and held their breath at the tip. They continued the sequence along every finger, finishing at the base of the pinkie finger, moving up and down like a roller-coaster.

"Thanks," Amy said sheepishly, her head bowed.

Mrs Gallen, Amy's teacher, was a frail old woman who seemed to grow greyer and slower as the school day grew shorter. She scratched the wiry hairs on her chin and surveyed the pair before her.

"Page nine, everyone, please," Mrs Gallen began, "Equivalent fractions this morning, a piece of cake for those who can remember their times tables. Miss Cupples, I don't want Mr Hannaway to feed you answers. Please take the empty seat in the corner, next to my coat. I do hope you've been practising."

"Ah, Miss, come on, I know them. I swear," Amy lied. "I don't need to move."

Mrs Gallen remained stern-faced and silently pointed to the empty chair.

Amy hated numeracy work, especially anything that involved multiplication. She trudged across the room, choosing to ignore Conor's fake laugh, and slumped into her new seat.

Amy's eyes stared across at Jamie and his messy black hair. He caught her gaze and, for a moment, held it. He continued to show the breathing technique and smiled.

"Pssst!" came a sound from behind Amy. "Pssst!"

"Focus on your work, please," snapped Mrs Gallen without looking up.

Amy whipped her head around to the wall behind her, only making her look more guilty.

In the corner of the classroom, behind Amy's seat, hung a small circular mirror next to a hook where Mrs Gallen hung her thick purple coat.

Her eyes were naturally drawn to the mirror. It couldn't be, could it?

"Oi, Amy!" came a whisper. Then a waving hand was thrust through the mirror and into the classroom.

The shocked girl leapt from her seat, "A hand!" she yelled.

"I will indeed give you a hand," replied Mrs Gallen. "But please remain in your seat and don't shout out."

As the teacher approached, Amy could hear chuckling from the mirror.

After ten minutes of over-explaining and frowning at how little Amy knew, the teacher began meandering between tables and looking over shoulders to inspect books.

"Jamie," barked Mrs Gallen. "Get that phone up to me now."

"But Miss"

"Now, Mr Hannaway! My desk!"

"But Miss, I wasn't…"

"Excuse me?! Do not have me repeat myself!"

"But Miss, I didn't…"

"One more but from you and you'll not see that mobile phone for a very long time."

"Big butts!"

The class erupted into laughter, and a vein on the side of the teacher's head began throbbing violently. Jamie, of course, was not stupid. He did not say this extra 'butt.' Much to Amy's horror, it came from behind her, from the mirror, from CD, no doubt!

Mrs Gallen didn't react. Her deathly stare silenced the class. She calmly pointed to her desk and said one word before sitting down, "Phone!"

"It wasn't me, Mrs Gallen," pleaded Jamie. "It came from…..he paused…..over there," he added, pointing in Amy's direction.

Jamie walked towards his teacher with his head hanging and placed the mobile phone down. Only one other head in the room hung lower, Amy's.

12
Colourful Shirt

Amy marched out of class with a scowl and headed straight for the toilets. CD was proving useless to date. He wouldn't help to rescue the missing children and he had just caused Jamie to have his mobile phone confiscated.

She checked the cubicles for other girls and then returned to the door. It wouldn't lock, though, the latch was broken, and the door itself squealed out in pain as it was forced closed.

Amy paced the length of the room, knocking on every mirror above the sinks as she did so. Unsurprisingly, CD didn't arrive. Perhaps he had seen the look on her face and decided better of it.

Even lunchtime and a chat with Jamie didn't change Amy's mood much.

"I know it wasn't you," Jamie reassured her. "Those from The Reflection need to be watched. Do you think that boy will be back? Would the other beasts come to our school?"

"I really don't know," she replied solemnly. "But he's going to make up for it, I promise."

The afternoon lessons dragged by even slower than the morning. Amy was frequenting the toilet so often that her teacher was becoming concerned. And two younger girls who happened to see her knock-on mirrors and speaking to herself laughed her out of the toilets.

When the home time bell finally sounded, the flutter in her chest grew with anticipation. The plan was easy; get home, scold CD then allow him to make up for it by helping to rescue the children.

But Amy didn't have to wait until she got home. On exiting the school building and heading towards the mass of parents at the gates, she could hear someone screaming her name over and over. She turned towards the playground to see CD bounding towards her and Jamie, wearing a grin and looking sickeningly pleased with himself. Amy clenched her fists; her cheeks smartened and glowed crimson.

"Oh, so now you show up," she said, dripping with attitude.

"I take it my little butt joke didn't go down too well?"

Amy didn't reply. She stood still and stared, straight-faced and tight-lipped.

"I suppose it wasn't the best timed," stated Jamie.

"Don't speak to him, Jamie. He owes you an apology first," Amy insisted.

"For what?"

"For what? For what?" blurted Amy, exasperated, her eyes narrowed on CD. "Thanks to you, Mrs Gallen has Jamie's mobile."

"Okay, okay," said CD. "I'll sort it. Don't worry."

"Jamie! Jamie! Over here!" came a holler.

"I had better go. There's my brother," said Jamie. "Try to get that phone back, please. If my brother ever demands it, I'm in trouble." Jamie darted off, leaving Amy muted as CD continued to pull on his jumper in a fruitless attempt to stretch its length.

"Enough of the silent treatment. I can get it, easy. I'll go into The Reflecti..."

"Sshhh," Amy interrupted. "There's Grandad."

"One moment, mate," said Grandad, stopping momentarily to speak to his granddaughter. "Look, Jim, I'd best get on. But take my word for it. All the missing children will be back home soon. I can feel it in my bones."

Unsurprisingly, Grandad knew everyone. He almost made it his business to vet all the locals, to chat with them and find out their backgrounds. Mum said it was his mindset. He had worked in security for years and just couldn't switch off.

As they plodded towards home, with the sun hanging low in the sky, Amy awaited Grandad's interrogation of CD.

"Delighted! It's great to see Amy with more than just one friend."

"Grandad!" Amy growled, red-faced.

"So, young chap, what's your name?"

"He's CD," interjected the girl.

"Well, where are you from, CD?"

"I'm from…." he began, "a place just like this." He nudged Amy.

Both smiled.

"Ah well, that's the council estates for you. No individualism, just carbon copies of one another; one as boring as the next, full of the best people, though, that's for sure. Do you know, I think I might know your family, CD."

"I don't think…"

"You sound wildly familiar," interrupted Grandad. "I'm certain we've met before, haven't we?"

Amy glimpsed at Grandad's eyes. They were growing large with intrigue. She had to quash this sudden interest in her new friend.

"Is that a new shirt, Grandad?" she remarked.

Grandad brushed down his shirt covered in yellow leaves and smiled, "Ah, thanks. You know me. Got to have the clothes bright. They look best, don't you agree?" he continued before anyone could answer. "Do you know CD, I grew up in a place with little colour, so I swore I'd always kit myself out in colourful clothes. Ah, Davy, how have you been, old pal?"

As Grandad waved to another passer-by, Amy seized the opportunity to grab CD and race ahead. "See you at home, Grandad."

The pair darted inside and shot upstairs. Mum, still drilling, didn't even hear them arrive.

"So," began Amy, throwing CD onto her bed. "You were saying, about Jamie, fixing things?"

"Yeah, okay. I was thinking I could get the phone. Then you could give it back to him. It'll be like nothing ever happened."

"You mean go into The Reflection?" she asked, trying to contain her glee.

"Yeah, I'll go and get the phone from your teacher's desk and bring it back to you."

"I'll come too sure, in case you can't find it."

"The school? You?" croaked CD. "Not a chance. Way too dangerous. You couldn't possibly. That's where all the beasts are. They've been using it as a den."

It made sense to Amy, the vile creatures. Where do children congregate most? A school! "So they are close to a food source, I assume?" she asked.

"Of course not! They aren't stupid, these beasts. I thought you'd know that by now. No chance they would expose themselves. It's why they've survived so long. They use the school because it's the biggest building around. Enough space for every beast. They do it in every town they move through. Look, just stay here and be ready."   CD slid the towel back on the mirror like a curtain and stepped out of view.

The revelation of the beast's den did not deter Amy; a little smile revealed her teeth as she watched on. Where the beasts are, surely the kidnapped children are too!

13
Return the Mobile Phone

This wasn't just for Jamie, and it certainly wasn't for her. Amy was doing it for every boy and girl, every adult and child, and everyone and anyone who was living in fear. Dad had always told her that someone who watches a bully in action and does nothing is just as guilty. Well, this was the same. She had the poison, and she even had a guide in The Reflection, and above all, she had the courage. Amy wasn't prepared to sit idly by and do nothing. Her tummy was already tingling; the wait was agonising. Where was CD?

She paced the bedroom floor, counting the minutes go past. When he finally arrived, the street lights were on, and the smell of tonight's dinner wafted upstairs.

"About time!"

CD bent over double, panting and trembling. "Harder than I thought. I had to move slowly to stay out of sight."

"Well, did you get it?" Amy asked, impatiently slinging the water pistol around her finger like a cowboy in the Wild West.

CD pulled a mobile phone from his pocket, "Of course," he smiled. He took a deep breath, "So, you can just give this back to Jamie in school tomorrow."

"Tomorrow? No, no, he needs it now. What if his brother comes looking for it?"

"Fair enough," replied CD. "Is he coming to collect it?"

"Not quite; we're going to bring it to him," replied Amy.

"And how exactly are you going to manage that?"

She spun the gun around her finger again and nodded towards the mirror.

"No! Nope, not happening! We aren't doing it. You're not going back into The Reflection."

"Relax, CD, relax," Amy replied slowly and calmly. "I've got a plan."

"Ha! Doesn't matter. Coz, I'm not taking you."

Come on! You heard Jamie, his brother will kill him if he finds out he's lost his mobile already. And plus, I've got this!" she added, presenting the water pistol.

"And how's a tiny water gun gonna help us," he laughed.

"It's filled with poison. Told you Grandad could make it."

CD took the little plastic gun and examined it closely. "Unbelievable!" he gasped.

"I know. My Grandad's great, isn't he?"

"No, no, it's really unbelievable. I don't believe it. Some smell of it, looks like reflective dust, even sounds like it," he added, holding the gun to his ear. "But it simply can't be."

"Why not?" Amy asked indignantly.

"Only the Emperor and his family can control dust. No one else!"

"Well, maybe Crumlish is a relative of the Emperor because he told my Grandad the command," stated Amy.

"Did he now? Ha!" snorted CD. "Crumlish? No chance!"

"And how can you be so certain?" Amy hissed.

"Because I know Crumlish very well. And he's not related to the Emperor."

"He's alive?" she spluttered.

"Of course, he's alive."

"Well, I'm telling you, he told my Grandad the words. Dust from the Reflection, past Emperors, are thee."

"Heed my words and listen to me," interrupted CD.

"Wait, you know the command words too?"

"Of course I do," replied CD, pointing to his face. "I didn't always look like this."

Amy suddenly pressed her finger on the trigger of her poison-filled gun and stepped back. Lifford! He was human, a tactic to get close and snatch those the emperor really wanted.

"It was a punishment for helping humans," continued CD.

Amy's tense shoulders relaxed. She ran her fingers through her long red hair and sighed. "And a boy because it's the worst thing possible. It's what they eat, what they hunt. You'd be an outcast."

"Exactly!" agreed CD.

"Well then, here's a chance for some revenge. Come on!" Amy grabbed his hand. Her nostrils flared as she took one last breath, her chest heaving as she stepped into the mirror. The fire in her tummy was ignited. It flashed around her body, and she knew instantly that an ability was on the cusp of being revealed. She squeezed the poison pistol in her pocket and tried intensely to focus on the task.

"Aren't you cold?" CD asked, pulling the short sleeves of his red jacket down towards his wrists. "I mean, I'm used to it, and I still find it freezing."

Amy felt a breeze whip around her bare knees and neck, but she had no sense of whether it was cold. She glanced around her bedroom, noticing the thin dusting of frost on each surface.

"It's a bit of a strange one, but I don't feel the cold. Never have, well maybe before I was two years old. But I can't remember. You see, it's one of my abil...

"I told you, I know all about your abilities. About how your parents injected you with a new serum designed to cure illnesses and act as an antidote against poisons. But sadly, it had some unexpected side effects. I also know that Jamie and your parents are the only ones who know. And that your own Grandad has no idea. That's all well and good, but can we just get to Jamie's and get out of here? I'm assuming you know where he lives."

"Obviously," she replied, taking a hairband from her wrist to tie back her long, flowing red hair. "Just follow me."

"And what if we run into one of The Reflection's residents?"

"You mean a beast?" replied Amy.

"Perhaps, or worse, the emperor himself? What then? Use a little super ability? It'll take more than that."

"Look, we can cross that bridge when we get to it," replied Amy sharply.

"Bridge? This town has no bridges. Where are we going?" enquired CD.

"No, it means…it doesn't matter. Stop stalling, and let's go!"

The duo silently crept through Amy's room in The Reflection and made for the stairs. Even here, the second from the top stair moaned loudly when it stood upon.

Together they tentatively strode onto the muted street, the only sound made by their pounding hearts. Beads of sweat tickled down Amy's forehead. Judging by the visible breath expelled with every pant, outside was even colder than indoors. A blackish moss layered the footpaths making it slippery underfoot. The grass, patchy and dying, was frozen. The deserted street looked like an abandoned area after a nuclear fallout. The houses sat lifeless, and the neglected dust-covered cars resembled carcasses lining the road.

"Wait," Amy whispered, feeling like she was about to faint. "Why's it so deathly quiet?"

"Not a great choice of words. I don't want to even think about death. Let's get this done and get home."

From his tone, CD feared the beasts, probably more so than Amy. She began to understand why. Living as a human in a world where they are nothing but prey, in constant fear for his safety, it's like a zebra trying to feel at home in a lion enclosure. And considering that a lion eats up to 40kg of meat daily, you can't blame the zebra for worrying.

14
Absence of Colour

"Stick to the shadows," stressed CD.

"I know, I know," Amy replied.

"And keep your voice down," he added. "Sshhh."

A sharp intake of cold air shocked the girl's chest as they moved into a fog that punctuated the rows of houses in the estate.

They pressed on, with Amy taking the lead. Together they weaved between gardens, crawled to stay below walls and tiptoed across the long, dead grass that crunched underfoot. With the school in sight, Amy quickened, trying not to look to Jamie's house on her immediate right.

The night was thick and dark, but a little light filtered down from the street lights overhead. The moon didn't shine its reliable, steady glow. It was faint, barely visible and hung like a suspicious eye in the sky just above the school.

"Where's Jamie's house?" asked CD. "Isn't this the way to school?"

"It's close, come on!"

CD suddenly grabbed Amy's arm and hauled her behind a low fence. "Look-Eyeries," he stated.

"On patrol. Looking for Reflectionists."

"Reflectionists? My Grandad has mentioned them. Do they wear all black and hunt beasts?" she asked, cautiously peeking between a gap in the wooden panels.

"How did you know?"

Amy pointed through the fence.

CD, like Amy, closed one eye and strained the other to look into the gloomy street. A solitary figure tracked the eyerie. The figure moved stealthily; from car, to tree, to wall; even managing to expertly conceal his lanky frame behind dustbins. Amy surmised it was a man from the figure's size and stance. He wore black overalls, buttoned from the waist to below the chin. The mysterious man carried an enormous double-barrel water pistol, the type with a shoulder strap. Amy knew instantly where she'd seen that gun before. And dangling on a hook around the man's waist was a long piece of dark fur.

Who was this figure? And where was he going? His identity was hidden behind a black mask and an oversized hood. Amy raised her eyes and dared to look over the fence. She was forcefully yanked back down.

CD's face wore an expression she had not seen before. He was pale, tearful and unblinking. Amy tore her eyes away from her companion's to look back upon the street.

A beast! A foul and undeniably evil beast was hot on the heels of the Reflectionist.

Amy froze, cemented to the dirt beneath her hands and feet. Yet she couldn't take her eyes from it as it lumbered forward. With a lump in her throat, she longed to call out a warning. A yelp, a scream, anything, but not a sound escaped.

"What are you doing?" whispered CD directly into her ear. "Stop it now! Before you get us caught."

Amy had held her breath and wore a vacant look on her face. She shrugged her shoulders and went to return her focus to the pursuit before her.

"Please, Amy, you've got to stop it," CD pleaded, pulling on her jumper.

Amy turned around slowly to face CD; only then did she catch her reflection in his eyes. Her own eyes were glowing blue. She knew instantly that this was another ability. A new ability she'd never exhibited before.

She grabbed CD and darted into the house at their rear. Once inside, she raced back to the window. She didn't need to wipe the window clear. Her vision was suddenly amplified like reindeer in the Arctic, whose golden eyes in the summer turn to blue in the dark winter months to capture more light. The once gloomy Reflection Street was now illuminated as if someone had suddenly turned on the big light.

CD began to shake her, "Breathe, Amy. In the nose, out the mouth. Argh, how does Jamie do this? What is it he does? You're going to get us caught. Cover your eyes or something!"

But Amy, silent and still, was fixated on the ghastly beast. Hunched over, it was still taller than the Reflectionist. As Amy stared in fascination, she compared the creature to the mythical yeti with a few adjustments. His body was muscular, covered with thin flowing dark fur, patchy in places and wet with sweat in others. The beast's two elongated arms almost

reached his knees. At the end of each arm were four abnormally long fingers, each topped with razor-sharp nails that twinkled like stars in a clear summer night sky. His arms, like his legs, bent twice. Each of his four limbs had two joints. The beast's feet were enormous, padded with thick skin underfoot- he moved silently, stalking the Reflectionist.

Suddenly the beast fell to all fours, like a gorilla, and advanced on the oblivious human. Amy could tell that he was moving at a frightening pace from how the beast's two little cat-like ears, perched high on his

head, were even flapping in the wind. The girl smacked the windowpane with the palm of her hand. Everyone and everything froze except the beast's ears. They twitched, and then in unison, both swung towards Amy's direction. The eyerie was suspended mid-air, the Reflectionist stopped, precariously balanced on a wall, and the beast had frozen mid-stride.

Slowly the beast's short neck rotated, and his beady little eyes scoured the scene. The Reflectionist turned on his heels and caught sight of the beast. The eyerie swivelled around and gave chase after the man who was now yards from confronting the beast. Amy, awestruck, could not fathom his bravery.

"Amy! Your eyes. Come on, do the breathing with me. You can relax. They're gone. So, please breathe." Amy didn't react. "I know, I know," he blurted. He withdrew the mobile phone, pressed play on music and thrust it towards Amy's left ear. "Music works, doesn't it? Calms you down. Listen, listen! Want to dance? That can help, too, right?"

CD began frantically hopping from one foot to the other. Then he placed a hand on Amy's shoulders and shook her. "You'll collapse if you don't breathe. And those torch eyes are gonna give us away."

Amy finally gasped for air, unaware she had been holding her breath the entire time. She looked at the clock on the wall. "That'll be the manatee. They can hold their breath for almost twenty-four minutes."

"Well, whoopie for them," CD replied sarcastically. "Can we just get to Jamie's and get out of here. I hate being in The Reflection."

"Okay," replied Amy solemnly, sensing the stress and worry in CD's voice and tense body. "Give me your hand."

She took his hand in hers, walked in a circle and then announced, "Ta-da! We're here." She tried hard to hold back the grin tugging at her cheeks.

CD marched over to a family portrait hanging above the fireplace and used his sleeve to wipe it clean. "You mean we've been here the whole time!"

"Surprise!" Amy smiled.

"Not cool, not cool at all. You knew this was his house. You were planning to walk right past it, just to get into that school. Look at the danger you put us in. You saw a beast. Now you know what to expect. Even if the missing children are in there, what could you do? And I say you, coz I'm not going near it. Just take this and get on with it." He tossed Jamie's mobile phone towards Amy.

Amy pressed the home button and illuminated the screen. Her heart swelled when she saw the picture.

The screen saver was a selfie of her and Jamie together, being silly and pulling faces. A huge grin landed on her face. But her expression quickly changed the more she stared at the phone. The colour was fading. She looked down at her school uniform. While seeming to be impossible, it was now even more horrible. The once rich brown jumper was now looking washed out and faded. Surveying the room, it too was absent of colour. The walls, curtains, settee, and even the plastic flowers next to the television were grey.

"It's this place," started CD."It sucks the colour and life out of things."

"Well then," Amy replied, "Let's get to Jamie's real room."

15
House Alarm

Amy felt different as she climbed upstairs and ventured towards Jamie's bedroom. She had seen things, beasts, and they could never be unseen. The determination and motivation to rescue the missing children swelled so much inside her that she was fit for bursting. Once the phone was returned, she would head straight towards the school on their journey home.

The room looked like Jamie's, with the superhero posters covering most walls and Star Wars ships dangling from the ceiling, but it was all barely visible beneath a layer of dust and frost.

"All we have to do now is go through that mirror and return Jamie's phone as he sleeps. Go check the coast is clear," she directed CD.

CD wiped clear a large mirror that rested on top of a chest of drawers and stuck his head through. "Sleeping like a baby, come on."

Amy put her hand in CD's and, using the pulled-out drawers like a little staircase, climbed into the mirror, out of The Reflection and into the real room. The warmth was instantly comforting. It reminded Amy of the time she visited Spain, stepped off the plane and was walloped straight in the face with a blast of warm air.

The bedroom was even more beautiful, especially for a comic superfan. It exploded with colour and vibrancy. Amy even noticed a new poster on the back of Jamie's door, '101 amazing animal facts.' Her chest heaved, and a smile grew upon her face.

She silently approached her best friend's bed and placed the mobile phone on top of a pile of books next to a can of orange juice. It was a random and varied book selection, including The Making of Star Wars, Train your dog, Cook with 5 Ingredients and Mathematics Made Easy.

"We don't need to go back into The Reflection," whispered CD, his hand on the bedroom door.

"No, wait! We can't! I need to return the way we came," Amy said eagerly.

"And why's that?" he replied with a sneer.

Amy suspected CD knew exactly why, "Because it'll be quicker to get home," she insisted.

"Okay," CD agreed surprisingly quickly.

"Really?"

"No!" CD threw Jamie's bedroom door open, sending it crashing into the wall. Jamie sprang up in his bed, eyes trying to focus. The hair on one side of his head was poker straight and stuck to his face, slightly hiding the orange drool rolling down one cheek.

"Mum? Dad?" called the drowsy boy.

Amy threw herself towards the open door and followed CD's cackle. The pair padded quickly along the thick cream carpet and down the stairs.

With no care for noise or subtlety, CD thundered through the house and out the front door.

BBBRRRrrriiiinnggggg!

The house alarm pierced the ears and shook to life the slumbering house. CD and Amy pelted towards home, not slowing the pace until the squealing alarm was just a faint beep in the distance.

It was becoming clear that CD would do anything to avoid being in The Reflection. Amy's hopes of getting him to join a rescue mission were fading fast, like candy floss in the rain. She'd have to be clever to get back into The Reflection.

16
Put up the Missing Posters

The next morning, Mum or Grandad did not need to nag incessantly for Amy to get up. But as she sat on the edge of her bed, it occurred to her that she possessed some abilities that could prove invaluable in The Reflection. Used in just the right way, she would have no problems rescuing the missing children, no matter how many fearsome beasts stood in her way.

But where was CD?

Approaching school, her accomplice still hadn't made an appearance. He'd surely not be in The Reflection. He detested the place. A sharp pang pierced Amy's stomach. Did the Emperor find out what she had done? Did the Emperor capture and punish CD?

She raced into school, excited to greet Jamie and his mobile phone and explain how she returned it to him.

But Jamie wasn't in class. He wasn't late either. He was absent. Lunchtime had rolled around, and neither CD nor Jamie was in school. Amy could feel a snake coil around her stomach and squeeze. It felt like all 6.25 metres of a reticulated python that had abandoned its South Asia home and was now residing inside her tummy.

Immediately after lunch, the entire school was summoned to the assembly hall. An unscheduled assembly usually meant a telling-off, but the tightening snake in Amy's stomach told her this was something more concerning.

Amy's class was the last to arrive. They nonchalantly sauntered past the entire school population, who sat silently on the floor. But not her class, not now; they were the elite. Now the oldest in the school, they moved through with a swagger and took pride of place on the benches at the back of the hall. But Amy's head remained hung low, heavy with worry.

The school principal marched purposefully onto the stage, and silence fell instantly. Whilst impossible, he appeared to rest his piercing eyes on every one of the children individually. Fear rolled down from the stage, like thunder clouds on the face of a mountain soaking the pupils. Mr Thomson, standing six and a half foot tall and weighing 20 stone of pure muscle, looked more like a wrestler. Any pupil or parent who dared cross him would be finished...1,2,3!

Mr Thomson had a wide and varied collection of teachers under his control. All were seated along the perimeter of the assembly hall, appearing as frightened of their boss as the children were.

There were, of course, the usual types that grace every school up and down the country; the sporty teachers, the scary teachers, the teachers who try to be funny, and the teachers who clearly want to be anywhere but in a school.

"Good afternoon, boys and girls."

"Good afternoon, Principal Thomson," droned the children in unison.

"As I am sure you are all aware, children, some of our friends are not in school today. Nor are they at home sick, on holiday or in hospital. For those of you who have seen the news or been told by your parents, we have had a spate of kidnappings lately. There is no easy way to say this, but some evil people are taking children without permission. Today we learned that our very own loveable Jamie Hannaway was taken last night."

A little screech escaped from Amy's throat before she could capture it.

The principal paused until the silence was resumed before continuing. He didn't have to wait long. "We at Barrack Street Primary School hold your safety and welfare as our primary concern. Do not walk anywhere alone, ensure you stay with crowds, don't talk to strangers and only go home if you are with an adult."

He strode side to side on the stage, ignoring the microphone and bellowed instructions that no soul dared to forget. He spoke calmly. "The police have the matter in hand and promise to return all missing children safely as soon as humanly possible. That is all, and thank you, now, back to class!"

Humanly possible? Amy gulped, *well there's your problem. You're not dealing with humans!*

As the assembly hall of children sat muted, Amy tried hopelessly to think of something else, anything else. She tried her breathing techniques and attempted to use her 5,4,3,2,1 grounding strategy. She even began singing to herself. She was woozy with worry, convinced that an ability would involuntarily reveal at any moment. With such a revelation, Amy couldn't fathom how she'd get through the rest of the afternoon. She wanted to race home, cry, hug her mother and hope she'd wake up from the nightmare.

But it was real. Compounded by the fact that they spent the last few hours in class making missing person posters to stick up in the local area. People were comforting Amy, offering condolences like she had a death in the family. Not one person had a bad thing to say about Jamie. And why would they? The remainder of the school day only served to make Amy more determined.

One protruding idea was stuck at the fore of her mind, an idea she couldn't remove- she needed to get back to The Reflection fast!

17
A Deadly Malteser

"Mum, did you hear the news? Jamie!"

Amy embraced her Mum, squeezing harder than she had done for a long time. She didn't care that she was among the oldest in school. She didn't care who was watching. School was over, and she just wanted Mum to make it all better. To say Jamie was okay, at home; just ill, and it had all been a misunderstanding.

"I did, my peanut. I can't begin to imagine how you're feeling. We'll go home, get some tea and have a nice chat."

Chat? thought Amy. *This was the time for action!*

"Where's Grandad?" asked Amy as she pulled free and wiped her face dry.

"He's at home. He said something about getting prepared," Mum sighed loud and obvious. "Whatever that means."

Preparing! About time! As the house came into view, the impatient girl raced on ahead. She almost blurted the news about CD and Jamie when she opened the door but was taken aback by the sight. Grandad was still in his purple pyjamas, on the sofa and hunched over the coffee table. Before him were tens of newspapers, all cut, trimmed and prepped for sticking.

"Ah, Amy, my darling, isn't it awful? You must be so upset," he said, reaching open arms to hug his granddaughter.

"So, you know about Jamie?"

"I do; it's all here in black and white. They've not given up their search for me either. Jamie's been the closest yet."

"I think it was my fault, Grandad," said Amy solemnly.

"It most certainly wasn't, Sweetheart. Poor Jamie is just the latest unfortunate victim. The report states the mirror in Jamie's room was scorched black, just like the other eight victims," continued Grandad. "They do that when they don't want to be followed. They'd break the mirror on the reflection side."

"You mean the mirror on top of the chest of drawers?"

"You know his room well," replied Grandad. The old man focused a steely gaze upon the girl.

Amy gulped down, settling her fizzy mind and untangling the growing knot of guilt in her stomach. She twitched as she pulled on the hairband wrapped around her wrist again. "Grandad, we might have help in The Reflection."

"What do you mean, child?"

Amy wasn't surprised that it didn't take much to persuade Grandad. For too long, he had been alone in his knowledge of the beasts' existence, but not any longer. He was practically salivating at the thought of CD being from The Reflection.

"How on earth did I miss it?" he hissed with clenched fists. "But you should never have trusted him, and you certainly should not have gone to The Reflection! And all to return a phone! I'm so disappointed in you."

That line, 'I'm so disappointed in you,' cut to the bone. A punishment would be better, even being yelled at.

"But I only went to look for the missing children," argued Amy. "I thought that once I was in The Reflection, I could help them escape, somehow."

"Too dangerous, Amy! The last thing I want in this world is to lose you."

"You won't. I'm fine, but doesn't that prove CD could be good, a friendly beast like the one you knew? I mean, we saw a beast in the Reflection, and he didn't take me to him."

"Not at all, my sweetheart. It tells me he's smart, a spy perhaps. Waiting for the perfect moment to take us both, I'd presume. I wouldn't be surprised if he were involved in taking your best friend. All too much of a coincidence. Don't you think?"

But the more Amy spoke of the events, CD and what they had done together, she was utterly convinced he was harmless. Even more than that, she was convinced he was there to help.

"No, Grandad, I don't believe that. He wouldn't. I know he's good. And I can prove it to you."

"Oh you can, can you?" Grandad replied whilst tossing a Malteser that he had withdrawn from a packet in his pocket.

Amy plucked the little chocolate ball from the air. A twinkle in her eyes danced. "I can, and when I do, we can all do something about the missing children and get Jamie back. We need to! Before it's too late. And we'll put to use all that poison you've made."

Grandad reclined back on the sofa, and his whole face lit up with pride. "Go on, tell me your plan," he said eagerly.

"We'll use this, this deadly Malteser."

Amy remembered using the reflective dust with Grandad and lacing the Maltesers with poison. It was an obvious plan; why hadn't she thought of it earlier?

"But that'll kill a beast? What if, like you say, CD is actually good?" said Grandad.

"Well, he'll be fine in that case," Amy assured him.

"What do you mean? There's poison in that Malteser, and we both know what it can do."

"Yeah, but don't you remember the command you gave the dust?" Amy began reciting the words

"Dust from the Reflection,

Past Emperors are thee,

Heed my words and listen to me.

I am your master. I command you to kill,

Evil beast from the Reflection, you can do it at will." Amy paused.

Grandad continued, with a smile, "A hit from you and the beast shall breathe no more,

Burn away, melt, damn them to the core. Of course, it will only kill evil beasts! I did that on purpose, you know," said Grandad.

"Sure, you did," Amy replied. "Sure, you did."

18
Grandad Knows

That night Amy tossed and turned for hours; theories, ideas and stories chased each other around her head. It didn't help to sleep with a plastic poison gun under her pillow. *Better safe than sorry.* But was it really necessary? CD had already taken her to The Reflection safely and home again. In fact, he always appeared most frightened of the beasts. *But then why hadn't he shown up? What had he to hide?*

Amy needed to get into The Reflection! Now more than ever. A fiery fury coursed through her every cell. She knew she could use each and every ability if she needed to. And if any beast dared to harm Jamie, she would not be held responsible for her actions.

It infuriated her that she couldn't get into The Reflection without CD. The frustration was amplified when she thought of Jamie in there, alone, scared, cold and crying for help. So, the moment CD passed a little test in front of Grandad and was shown to be a good beast, they'd be off to rescue everyone.

Every time Amy's heavy eyes threatened to drift into a slumber, her worried mind was awoken by Grandad leaving his room. She woke with a start and instinctively leapt towards her door only to hear the pop of the toilet light spring into action.

Grandad was forever making toilet trips at night; Amy had already counted five so far. She wished she could have the ability of a giraffe and survive on only two hours of sleep a day.

She couldn't sleep. Perhaps the digital clock on her bedside cabinet was broken; the minutes didn't seem to pass. She peeked through a broken blind into the deserted street. The night was thick and dark, and every house was in complete darkness. Amy climbed from her bed and tiptoed downstairs to find Grandad in the kitchen. He was spritely and chipper, despite the time. She glanced at the clock ticking on the wall that read 2:34am. He was munching happily on a fried egg sandwich and sipping tea. The moment Amy entered the room, there was a seriousness in his voice, an urgency.

"You didn't wake me; I assume he didn't show up?"

Amy shook her tired head.

"That says it all, Amy, a sure sign of guilt. We had ourselves a lucky escape with him."

THUMP

"What was that?" asked Grandad.

THUMP

"Mum? Maybe. She'll go nuts if she finds me out of bed."

"No chance, my love," replied Grandad. "Your mum claimed my snoring was keeping her up. So, she invested in some earplugs. She's out like a light up there."

"The noise is upstairs; if it's not, Mum," rushed Amy. "It'll be him! I told you, Grandad. I bet he rescued Jamie. Maybe he's with him." She made haste and took the stairs in a single bound. Like a snow leopard jumping over fifteen feet, the length of a bus. Her grandfather was left shuffling behind.

"You really should tidy this room," moaned CD picking himself up off the floor. "I could have broken a bone just then."

"Perhaps we'll leave a little run-way for you in front of the mirror," interjected Grandad, brushing Amy aside and entering the bedroom. "How is The Reflection nowadays?"

CD stood silent, open-mouthed. His breath came in short gasps. Amy was equally as pensive. But she was focused on Grandad's comment. 'The Reflection nowadays he said, nowadays!' He must have been there. He had to be the Reflectionist who chased the beast.

"Ha, ha, good one, Charlie," CD chuckled nervously.

"He knows," said Amy.

"He does?" squeaked CD.

"He does," interjected Grandad. "He knows everything."

"Well then, Charlie, you know I'm here to help you. I've kept loads of eyeries from you already. And I can keep many more."

Grandad stood with a clenched fist around his new walking stick and a furrowed brow, his stare fixed upon CD. "Did you think you'd get away with it, young lad, hey? Swanning up here and playing us all for fools before you whisk us off."

CD looked puzzled. Turning to Amy, he shrugged his shoulders.

"He thinks you're planning to snatch us for the Emperor, and he thinks you were involved in taking Jamie."

CD sighed loudly, "What? No! Are you mad? I'd never! But with Jamie, I think we may both be slightly to blame."

"What are you getting at? Explain yourself!" demanded Grandad.

"Well, I think they followed us, Amy. I think that's how they found Jamie."

Amy hung her head. Her chest heaved heavily, and her shoulders collapsed towards her feet.

"But I swear, Charlie, I had nothing to do with it," insisted CD.

Grandad tore his eyes from his distraught granddaughter and shuffled threateningly towards CD.

Amy interrupted quickly, "Look, just eat this," she said, offering a solitary chocolate treat. "Then we can get on with rescuing Jamie and the others." She tossed the Malteser across the room in CD's direction.

Without hesitation, CD fell to one knee and expertly caught the sweet in his open mouth. With one squish between his teeth, he swallowed and opened his mouth to reveal that the contents were gone.

Grandad reached for Amy's hand and stepped back towards the door. Amy, eyes fixed upon CD, didn't budge.

19
It's me, Charlie

Nothing happened. No fizzle. No disintegration. No messy goo remains.

"Are you happy now, Charlie? Can you both stop being weird? I don't even like chocolate."

Amy nudged the old man and flashed an enormous grin in his direction.

"Hold on, young chap, where do you get off calling me Charlie? A bit of respect, please."

"But we know each other, Charlie," replied CD. "We've known one another for almost half a century."

Grandad stuck his tongue out and traced it along his lower lip in that considerate way old people seem to when they are deep in thought. "We have?" he asked, finally.

"It's me, Charlie, Crumlish!"

"Crumlish?" screeched Amy. "The same Crumlish that Grandad met as a boy?"

"The same one," he replied. "The one who saved your Grandad from eyeries. And now I'm saving his grandchild too. I was going to tell you sooner, but after Lifford turned up as a human, I saw how on edge you both were. There was no way your Grandad would allow you to trust another beast, especially one who had been turned human."

The atmosphere in the room completely changed in an instant. Grandad's paranoid state and over-protectiveness eased, his shoulders relaxed, and the hand fiddling with the sweet packet in his pocket ceased.

"I thought you were dead," exclaimed Grandad. "How did I miss it? I should have known it was you. This is exactly why I'm retired. I'm not what I used to be."

"Don't beat yourself up, Charlie. It was a long time ago. And I did look very different back then. This was a punishment," said CD, pointing to his face, "for helping you. Emperor Cashel was all set on getting revenge and killing you fifty years ago. But he couldn't get to you when I squashed the eyeries and broke your mirrors from The Reflection side. So he did this to me. Worse than death, he said. Then he called me Crumlish Doyle, just to mock me further."

"That's Grandad's surname," blurted Amy. "So that's where CD came from. How did he turn you human?"

"The same way he did with Lifford, using reflective dust."

"I know how that feels," muttered Grandad.

"Ehey?" said Amy.

"The reflective dust, I know how it feels to use it."

"Yeah, I've been meaning to ask you about that," remarked Crumlish. "Just how do you know so much about The Reflection and the dust? I certainly never told you. The less you knew, the better, in my opinion."

"Err, amm," stuttered Grandad.

"You've been, haven't you?" spluttered Crumlish excitedly. "You've got Lifford's toe, and you used it to get into The Reflection. That's it, isn't it?"

I knew it! thought Amy. It was all so obvious. Grandad had to be that Reflectionist she had seen; it was the dead beast's toe she had spied hanging from his belt!

"Let's use it then, Grandad," exclaimed Amy. "Lifford's snapped off toe, and the poison, to rescue everyone."

"And I've found them!" announced Crumlish. "Jamie too. That's where I've been all day. They're trapped in the school. I think they followed me when I went to Jamie's house."

"They probably thought he was my grandchild," Grandad added. "Makes sense, I suppose. If they know that you helped me once, they may have thought you were at it again."

"But, Charlie, I think young Amy might be right," began CD. "Maybe you should do something about it. Whilst they are still alive."

"Don't you mean we should do something about it?" stated the determined girl with bright eyes.

"I can't. It's far too dangerous," Grandad argued. "And anyway, I gave away Lifford's toe. I don't have it anymore."

"Not to worry," chirped Amy. "We don't need it. We've got CD, I mean Crumlish. And I've got a plan."

20
The Reflection School

"Don't you do anything you're told?" said Crumlish, shuffling his feet as he paced around the bedroom. "Bad enough you didn't keep the mirror covered when he asked, but this, this is going too far."

"Technically, Grandad said that he couldn't go. He didn't say we can't," replied Amy, grinning as she pulled on her woolly school jumper and trainers. "We need to. Jamie needs us, now!"

"I can't," spluttered Crumlish. "This is ridiculous. He'll be furi..."

"Look," interrupted the eager girl. "Jamie would bend over backwards to help me. So, I intend on doing the same."

"Bend over backwards?" questioned Crumlish. "That sounds painful. How would..."

"No, it means that...it doesn't matter." Amy snatched Crumlish's arm and hauled him into the mirror, leaving an empty room and Grandad still peeing in the toilet next door.

As they meandered between houses and through gardens, Amy wasn't convinced it was her estate. Many of her older neighbours had beautiful gardens filled with blooming flowers that poetically bobbed like hundreds of balloons at a birthday party. The houses themselves were a welcoming dash of multicolours—one red, the next yellow, blue, then green. The pattern was random, but clearly, the residents had collectively agreed upon a colour each.

But that was the real world. Now she was in The Reflection, and every house had virtually lost all its colour.   The flowers were withered and grey. The lawns were balding and crunched underfoot.

Nearing the school, the situation didn't improve. Practically all of the windows were broken, and those that weren't had been covered with pieces of rotting cardboard. A faint glow of light showed life on the ground floor of the building; upstairs, in darkness, looked vacant.

"I still don't see why you couldn't force Charlie to come too," said Crumlish, annoyed at Grandad's absence. "I know he's your Grandad, and you love him, but it's all a bit suspicious, considering things he knows."

Amy silently agreed, but she would never let it be known. She would defend her Grandad to the end because, if asked, he'd do the same for her. "It wouldn't make sense. Jamie and the rest are alive for a reason. The Emperor hasn't got what he wants yet- my Grandad. And let's say he got caught. Then what use would having the children be? They'd all be killed for certain."

"Hmm, I suppose." Crumlish stopped as they neared the school gates, one of which had been yanked off and lay on the ground. "I just don't think this is a great idea. At least you've got the poisonous water gun to protect you. And all those special abilities. What have I got?" He kicked the dirt on the ground and started walking back toward where they came, his knees knocking.

"Look, you take this," said Amy, offering the poison pistol. "We need each other. Now, let's stick to the plan."

Amy had to take the lead. Crumlish was so different in The Reflection. She had seen him being bold, even cheeky. But in The Reflection, he was frightened and, at worst, cowardly.

She grabbed his forearm and patted him on the back. "We can do this!"

21
Dinner Time

The duo cautiously crept along a shadowy corridor. With every step, they neared a beastly hum ahead. Crumlish was shaking so much that Amy thought something would fall off. Her eyes darted around the wall displays that were all absent of colour and then down to her jumper, which was once a deep rich brown. It now resembled a piece of out-of-date chocolate. The lack of colour only added to the dread that sank its teeth into her bones.

"The kids are near," Crumlish whispered. "I saw them in the classroom, just around the next corner."

"What's that ahead?" Amy spotted a dull amber light spilling out from the canteen. "Are they eating?"

Crumlish looked at the dark skies through the dirty window. "I think so. It's that time. Now come on! And stay down."

Now crawling, they stealthily ventured below the windows, looking into the canteen. Amy swept away the tufts of dark hair that littered the school floors like confetti.

"It's them," whispered Crumlish. "They shed."

Amy shuddered. But this little nugget of new information only piqued her interest further. She slowly raised her head to look through the window.

"STOP WHAT YOU ARE DOING!"

bellowed a voice from the canteen.

Crumlish and Amy both froze. Their heartbeats thumped in unison and echoed around the corridor.

"Please, move!" Crumlish pleaded with an undeniable tone of desperation in his voice. He slithered on in silence.

"Who's that?" whispered Amy.

"The Emperor."

"Emperor Cashel?" the girl asked brightly.

A cacophony of sounds seeped from the room. Amy had to look. A burning ball in the pit of her stomach willed her to. Tentatively she craned her neck and peeped through the cloudy glass into the canteen. Her heart stopped, rested, and then pounded harder and faster than ever, smashing against her ribcage. Like a little pygmy shrew whose heart beats over one thousand times a second, her mouth fell open as the full impact of what she saw hit her.

The beasts were even more ghastly than she remembered. Perhaps it was the dull lighting above that reflected off the shiny bald patches in their fur or the fact there were so many in one place, but Amy couldn't take her eyes off them. Their fur resembled shades of human hair; blacks, greys, blondes, browns; all shades but all fading. And that's where the similarities ended.

Emperor Cashel, rested at a table, alone, along the back wall of the canteen whilst all the other beasts squeezed uncomfortably around children-size tables, adding only to the illusion that they were truly enormous. The Emperor was dark and frightening, with a silhouette alone that could induce nightmares. His stretched face was long and gaunt with distinguishing harsh bony features. His eyes were enormous and hauntingly black, and two stumpy ears rested upon his head. The emperor was covered in a distinguished black fur, with flecks of silver scattered throughout. Like the other beasts, on the floor around him lay fur that had been shed. The emperor was undoubtedly bigger and stronger than the rest, his yeti-like body looked solid, with bulging muscles and thick arms.

"I want the beast responsible up here now!" boomed Emperor Cashel in a voice that shook the room.

One cowering beast was suddenly pushed towards the Emperor. His soft padded feet did little to stop his motion forward. The room vibrated with awkwardness. The silence was threatening, tense and long. Emperor Cashel eventually stood up from his seat. His sheer height took Amy aback. He towered over the other beast before him. As he came into full view, the girl gasped at the sight of a thick terrifying tail that followed the emperor. A tense tail poised to strike like a deathstalker scorpion, the deadliest of all scorpions.

"Aren't you meant to protect my Anywhere Mirrors?" Emperor Cashel asked slowly and threateningly.

"Yes," the beast began tremblingly, "I am, Master. I'm Killead."

"I don't care who you are!" barked Emperor Cashel. "I was told the beast tasked with protecting my mirrors was clever. I was told they'd be safe in his possession. I was told you'd never let a Reflectionist get one of my Anywhere Mirrors." Each 'I was told' line was spat out like venom and got louder on every occasion. Suddenly, and without warning, Emperor Cashel stooped his head like a bull and charged. Amy even flinched. The enormous emperor was going to run right through him. But then he slammed on the brakes, dug the end of his razor-sharp tail into the floor and loomed over the trembling beast.

Emperor Cashel relished the power he had. In a single movement, he pulled his tail from the ground and coiled it around the body of Killead. He raised him high into the air like a puppy lifted by the scruff of the neck. Dangling, completely vulnerable, the unfortunate beast blubbered as the Emperor moved his face uncomfortably close, resting his unforgiving eyes upon him.

"I was told wrong," hissed the Emperor. Spit was expelled with every word. "You're useless!"

"It...it w..w..won't happen again," Killead stuttered. "It won't, Master."

"That's the first correct thing you have said, and it's your last."

Emperor Cashel twisted open a mirrored orb that dangled from a thick chain around his neck. He emptied some of its contents onto his claw. *Reflective dust!* Even from this distance and through a murky window, the stuff shone like a sky of stars. Amy quickly cupped her hands around her eyes to test for a blue shimmer. Her vision was so good that it had to be an ability. If not the deer, she surmised it must have been the cheetah DNA in her blood again exhibiting itself. Besides running fast, the large cat can spot prey five kilometres away.

Emperor Cashel raised the dust to his mouth, whispered some words, then purposefully and cruelly tipped the dust slowly over Killead. The beast howled and screeched in a way Amy had only heard once before - Lifford! He slowly melted away into a sticky black mess that released small plumes of smoke.

"Now, find that mirror!" roared Emperor Cashel. "You know it won't be far."

The beasts rose from their seats when a **clip-clop,**

clip-clop sound silenced them. A collective gasp engulfed the canteen, and they all stood motionless.

"Ahh, you made it. Wonderful!" announced Emperor Cashel.

A pain stung Amy's chest, and an overwhelming sweet smell tinged her nostrils. A few beasts could be seen retching and gagging.

It couldn't be. Could it? Amy stood on her tiptoes, bounced up and down, and even considered sneaking into the canteen. She needed the beasts to sit down! She needed to see who it was!

"If I had competent beasts," began Emperor Cashel, addressing the beasts before him, "then I wouldn't need to bring in a…." he paused, "..let's call her a consultant."

Amy could feel beads of sweat gathering again on her forehead, but she didn't dare lift a hand to wipe them away. With a steely focus, her eyes pierced the back of the beasts. Come on, move!

Suddenly she was yanked away from the canteen doors by Crumlish and forced further along the corridor.

"What are you doing?" complained Amy. "I needed to see…."

"Shhh, keep it down. You're going to get us caught. They'll be everywhere now searching for that Anywhere Mirror."

"What's that?"

"It's what it sounds like," Crumlish replied sarcastically. "A mirror that can go literally anywhere, not just into the room it's hung. They could be used to get into your house, Jamie's house, and even the White House. Emperor Cashel has a few of them.

Usually, he uses them to send eyeries through. Sometimes even for games."

"Games?" Amy asked, blinking blearily into the gloom ahead.

"Yes, now come on," Crumlish whispered forcefully.

"Relax, will you! Didn't you hear? The Reflectionists stole a mirror. They are probably here at this very moment, rescuing everyone."

"Ha, if only. But I'll gladly go home if you think that's the case," CD said, stopping to look Amy in the eye. "They won't have gotten far. The further an Anywhere Mirror gets from the Emperor's orb, the heavier it becomes. It'll be somewhere close. And they'll find it if they don't find us first, that is. Now, please, can we go," he pleaded, his voice wavering.

The view out the window was dreary and depressing. On one side, Amy had horrid skies and on the other wretched beasts. She had seen what Emperor Cashel could do. The beasts were as clever as they were evil. *Maybe this wasn't a great idea.*

22
Saggart Twins

Together they wormed their way along, when Amy suddenly broke into a sprint and motored down a long stretch of corridor.

"Quick! I can hear them! Come on!" she called over her shoulder.

The muffled sound of children crying grew louder with each step taken. But Amy's excitement was abruptly halted when a thunderous deep belly laugh drowned out the cries. She paused short of turning the corner and allowed Crumlish to catch up.

In a fumbling panic, he dropped the plastic gun filled with poison and shrank further into the shadows holding his breath.

"I knew it," he whispered. "Saggarts."

Amy looked to Crumlish, whose eyes were almost nothing but white. "What's a Saggart?" she asked.

"Massive beasts, the biggest, twin brothers. Not the brightest but huge. They are blocking the door. Ah, well, we should just give up now. They'd kill us for sure. Let's go before we're seen."

Amy discreetly peeked around the corner. The enormous Saggarts came into view. Every time they moved, their bald cone heads scraped the ceiling, sending clumps of plaster towards the ground. Amy clocked the size of the four fingers on their hands like bunches of sharpened, rotten black bananas. Every ounce of blood in her body instantly sank to her feet. Her head felt light and floaty, and she thought that one little nudge would topple her over.

"We're so close. We can't stop now! We're not stopping now! My best friend is in there." She bit her bottom lip and stared at the ceiling. "Look, you said they aren't too clever, right?"

"Right, idiots, in fact."

"Well then, I've got a plan. Invisibility- ghost shrimp."

"You've always got a plan," replied Crumlish, rolling his eyes.

Crumlish listened intently before admitting, "I can't believe I'm going to say this, but that might actually work."

Amy's eyes sparked as she stepped into the shadows and removed her school uniform. Each item of clothing was tossed at Crumlish, who quickly put it over his clothes.

"I'm not sure this is going to catch on," he remarked, looking down at the brown pleated school skirt over his dirty joggers.

Now completely and utterly invisible, Amy stood beside Crumlish and giggled, startling him.

"Right, you know what to do. I'll stay close. Just stick to the plan," whispered Amy.

"Okay, I will," Crumlish agreed reluctantly.

Together they tentatively turned the corner and into the view of the Saggarts. Their bony elongated faces and dopey eyes were slow to react or notice the new arrival. Eventually, their open mouths produced some sounds.

"What do you...?" roared the Saggart on the right.

"Want?" finished the Saggart on the left.

Every word projected was accompanied by the most diabolical of smells. Amy wrinkled her nose in disgust. Emotions fuelling invisibility were clearly impacting her sense of smell. Surely no creature could have breath so bad. It must be the bear's amazing nose. They have a sense of smell one hundred times that of a human.

"I...I...I.. have orders from the Emperor," stuttered Crumlish. "To question the children."

"Question the children?" said the Saggart on the left.

"Why?" asked the Saggart on the right.

"Isn't it obvious?" he replied. "Don't you know who I am?"

"Of course we do," said the Saggarts in unison. "You're Crumlish"

A sly little grin grew upon Crumlish's human face. The recognition gave him a little boost of confidence and made his chest puff out a little further.

"Who else would have an ugly human face?" they laughed. Crumlish was crestfallen.

"But why.." began the Saggart on the right.

"You?" finished the other.

"Because they'll trust me. With this face, I'm one of them. You see, it has its benefits being one of only two beasts ever turned human by the Emperor."

"You mean one of three," stated the Saggart on the right.

"See, idiots," Crumlish whispered to Amy. "No, there's Lifford and me. That's it." He spoke in a slow, condescending fashion, emphasising every word.

"You're wrong," the Saggart on the left began.

"There was another one, just over fifty years ago, that happened before you," finished the Saggart on the right.

"Okay, whatever you say," dismissed Crumlish. "Look, are you going to let me in?"

"Maybe, but why are you..."began the Saggart on the left.

"Dressed like a human poo?" laughed the other as he stooped down.

Amy was unable to look away from the pair of

Saggarts. The bald patch in their leather-like skin shimmered in the flickering fluorescent light above. And yet, as they moved closer, Amy saw a naivety behind their eyes.

"It's the school uniform belonging to some of the children," announced Crumlish in a tone that appeared much braver than he felt. "Emperor Cashel wants more information. Scaring them to death isn't working, so this is a new tactic."

"That makes sense," said the Saggart on the right.

"Isn't the Master clever?" added the Saggart on the left.

"But scaring them is fun," said the Saggart on the right.

"I agree," chuckled the other. "And it makes them taste delicious."

"Speaking of things being delicious, my questioning could take a while. Emperor Cashel said you can join the rest for food while I carry out the investigation," lied Crumlish.

The word 'food' was still hanging on his lips, and the Saggarts were already plodding down the corridor.

"Well played, Crumlish," said Amy, patting his back. "That worked perfectly. You were right; they aren't very clever."

"You said it," he agreed, pointing, "Look, the key's still in the door."

23
Tight Hug

A solitary flickering light dimly lighted the classroom. All the desks were pushed together, blocking the door, and the children were huddled at the back of the room. Screams and shuffling began to ensue the moment the door was forced open, just wide enough for Amy and Crumlish to squeeze through.

Crumlish quickly removed the school uniform and held it out. Amy snatched the bundle and scuttled off to the corner to dress.

"You're still invisible," stressed Crumlish, seeing a floating brown uniform return to his side.

"Reach over your goals; believe in victory," whispered Amy.

"Very motivational," drawled Crumlish. "But it's not the time."

"No, it's an acronym."

"Bless you," replied Crumlish.

"I didn't sneeze. An acronym. It's a way to help me remember the colours of the rainbow. Reach over your goals, believe in victory. Each word starts with the letter of colours in the rainbow. Then I search for an item of each colour. It's a grounding technique, helps calm me down, controls my emotions and abilities."

"Get on with it then!"

"It's not easy. This place is so dull. Everything is faded." Amy strained her eyes and looked around the dark classroom. Her eyes began to illuminate with a tinge of blue. "Red jumper, orange display wall, yellow pencils on the floor, green shoes," she said, nodding towards Crumlish's feet.

"Whatever you're doing, it's working," smiled Crumlish. "Now come on. Let's rescue this lot and get out of here."

Amy slowly threaded her way towards the victims. Cowering tight together, no one dared raise a head or glance in her direction. Her stomach bubbled with nerves. *Were they all still there? Had anyone been harmed?* She tentatively neared the group only to see the huddle retreat further into the darkness.

"Jamie," she called out. **"Jamie! Are you there?"**

One boy slowly rose to his feet. Dishevelled and exhausted, he stumbled forward, "Who is it? Amy? Is that you?"

Amy watched as the boy strained his eyes and stepped into the light. Despite the baggy eyes, red cheeks and hoarse voice, there was no denying it was Jamie. Burning guilt sparked in her tummy after seeing her best friend.

Amy raced forward, straight into his open arms. Her eyes welling, she squeezed him tightly.

"Errr...stop...Amy...I can't breathe," gasped Jamie.

"Sorry, Jamie. Are you okay? Have they hurt you?"

Jamie's teeth were still chattering when a little girl stepped from behind him into the light.

"Did they get you, too?" she asked, looking at Amy.

Amy noticed how the little blonde-haired child hopped from one foot to the other and had her pyjama sleeves pulled down over her hands. She immediately removed her school jumper and pulled it over the child's head.

"Amy, this is Minnie," began Jamie. "And they didn't get her." He smiled. "No chance they'd get Amy! She's here to rescue us."

"You mean take us home?" Minnie asked tentatively.

Suddenly the children, who had not heard a mention of home in days, weeks for some, began to swarm together like moths beneath the light.

Amy stared out a window into the thick dark night before clearing her throat. "Right, everyone, let's get out of here." She reached up and opened the latch, allowing a screaming cold wind to break in.

A collective gasp enveloped the room, and the children swiftly moved closer together.

Amy, Crumlish and Jamie ushered the traumatised group towards the window. They exchanged a small but encouraging nod as they began their daring escape.

Suddenly the classroom door flew open with such force that four tables were sent sailing across the room. The children instantly began wailing and shrank back into a dark corner. Amy and Crumlish froze, statue still at the sight before them.

24
Bravery over Fear

"Well, well, well," purred Emperor Cashel, filling the door frame. "Going somewhere?"

The light spilling in from the corridor threw an emperor-shaped shadow across the room, plummeting the trembling children into darkness. He stooped to enter, the two Saggarts at his rear.

Slowly and menacingly, the enormous Emperor Cashel crossed the grimy tiles. He flicked the plastic covering on the flickering light as he passed. It stayed on momentarily before flickering again. Dark then light, each time Emperor Cashel came into view, he loomed closer then closer still, making the children shudder.

Amy's determined eyes were fixed upon those of the emperor. They were unfathomably black, large, and almost hypnotic, sunken into his long face. The winking light reflected off the orb around the emperor's neck. As she was drawn in for a closer look, Amy considered that it worked like the luminous appendage dangling at the front of an angler fish's head. Despite living in the darkest depths of 30,000 feet below the ocean's surface, unsuspecting victims were attracted to the light. Before it was too late, she finally tore her gaze away to focus on Crumlish, who was making a sound like air escaping a balloon in his attempt to speak.

"You are a tiresome little beast," mocked Emperor Cashel. "You didn't actually think it would work, did you?"

The emperor began pacing the room and circling the children. With every step, the orb swung like a pendulum in a massive grandfather clock. The thudding sound ticked like a bomb, ready to explode. As one, the children moved to avoid the sinister emperor and soon found themselves centred in the room.

Amy spotted Crumlish frozen, open-mouthed terror, with the poison pistol still in his hand. She instantly threw an elbow into his side. He dropped the gun. Their eyes followed the blue plastic gun as it bounced to rest against the emperor's foot. Without looking, he kicked it to the side.

"I..I...I...can explain," chirruped Crumlish.

"Speak up," barked Emperor Cashel. "Speak up, you good-for-nothing creature."

Crumlish looked to Amy with regretful eyes, then turned back to Emperor Cashel, "You see this child, this girl is..is…is…"

"Quiet, you stuttering fool! Get over with the other nine pathetic humans." Emperor Cashel paused and scanned the children. "Ten? I thought there were nine. Ha! We've been taking so many children I've lost count," he chuckled. The two Saggarts to his rear began nervously laughing too.

Suddenly the emperor bent his knees and crouched down. He drew his face alongside Amy's, and sniffed with such force that his nostrils flared, and the ends of Amy's red hair were pulled into his nose like a vacuum cleaner.

"This one!" he barked. "This one!"

He knows, thought Amy. He knows I shouldn't be here. He knows Charlie is my grandad. She instantly clenched her teeth and chose bravery over fear.

"This one isn't scared!" stated Emperor Cashel. "Not scared in the slightest."

Amy held her breath and imagined calmly walking through the local forest, observing the wildlife and breathing in the fresh air. It helped instantly. On the outside, she looked cool and collected. But inside, her heart was thumping so hard she thought it might burst from her chest.

With every word from Emperor Cashel, his sickly green tongue rolled out of his mouth like an enormous snake trying to escape. Watching him was equally fascinating and horrifying, yet the sobbing children around her made Amy even more resolute in her decision to overshadow any fear.

"No, I'm not scared," piped up the defiant girl. She puffed out her chest and moved to the front of the group. **"Not of you or any other beast."** She had seen the shell of a person that fear had turned Crumlish into and refused to let it do the same to her.

"Not scared?" called one Saggart from the doorway. "Not good."

"No fear, no taste, Master. We need them to be scared," added the other. "Make them play mirror ball."

The two Saggarts howled with a deep bellied unpleasant laugh that shook the room.

The Emperor whipped his long neck around and silenced his accomplices with a deathly stare. An icy smile then stretched across the width of his face.

"Oh, you will be scared, child. You will be terrified!" announced Emperor Cashel, throwing his tail against the ground.

Crumlish shook his head, and his eyes fell to the ground.

25
Human Chain

"What's Mirror Ball?" Amy asked Crumlish as they regretfully trudged towards the assembly hall, the children following close behind.

Jamie was ushering the children along, whispering into their ears and comforting those in tears. He'd taken his position as the oldest with great gusto and compassion. It made Amy's heart swell with pride to have such a friend.

"It's a cruel game invented by the emperor for his amusement. Beasts versus humans."

"A cruel game? How? What's involved?" Amy gasped.

"It's a bit like football, I suppose, only you can use your hands too," Crumlish began. "Plus, there are five footballs per team. You have a net to defend and one to shoot into. Some players defend your goal, and the rest try to score."

Amy rolled her eyes. "What is everyone's obsession with football?"

"Ah, because it's the greatest game on earth," snorted Crumlish.

"Well, I hope you're good at this Mirror Ball."

"Oh, don't you worry, I'm good," gloated CD.

"You are?" Amy replied a little too quickly.

"Yes, I am," said Crumlish indignantly. "Well, I've never actually played. But I'm brilliant at football."

"Me too," interrupted Jamie. "I've been practising out my back garden, even did eight keep-ups last time. New record."

"But to be safe, you might need to use your abilities for this one," suggested Crumlish.

Jamie's eyes lit up. Amy took a long deep breath and began to fiddle with the hairband around her wrist.

Amy and the other children were used to a sports hall stinking a little after thirty red-faced children had finished a lesson, but this was on a new level. The assembly hall reeked. The smell was so vile that three children were pinching their noses, and a few could be heard retching. Not a single eye remained dry.

Stretched in a line on one end of the hall, the human team couldn't see their opponents. Twenty free-standing mirrors were scattered throughout the sports hall, each as large as a door. Every way Amy looked, she could see herself reflected from a different angle. And if she couldn't see herself, she caught sight of the trembling, sobbing children and Jamie's helpless attempts to comfort them. Her whole body was beginning to quiver. Amy's cheeks grew crimson, her brow furrowed, and a fire burst into flames deep in her stomach.

Emperor Cashel squatted on the stage, surveying the game. He was practically salivating at the thought of terrorising innocent young children in the name of entertainment.

"I see, so this is why it's called Mirror Ball?" stated Amy.

"But they aren't any ordinary mirrors. They're Anywhere Mirrors," drawled Crumlish.

"They're what?"

"Each mirror is linked to another. That one there," Crumlish pointed to the nearest mirror, "might be linked to a mirror right in front of the opponent's goal. Or you could be unlucky and run into one that will leave you outside this hall or even the whole school."

"More like lucky!" Amy beamed. "That's how we'll escape. We need to find that one!" The adrenaline spun around her veins like a race car on the tracks.

Amy's breathing suddenly increased violently, and with each short-panicked breath, she felt faint. She sighed loudly.

"What's wrong?" asked Jamie, seeing the look of horror on his friend's face.

"The plan, Jamie, it won't work," she said. "We need a beast's touch to get through mirrors."

Crumlish traced his tongue along his lower lip in thought, "I've got an idea," he stated as the whistle blew. "Play the game. Leave it to me."

Frantic thuds began bearing down on the group of children and their goal. The five children with a ball abruptly threw them away and clung to one another for dear life. Amy smashed one ball down the hall, wedged another under each arm and began to dribble a fourth in the direction of the opposition's net. Crumlish, upon seeing Amy, was shaken into life. He ran alongside her before veering off and leaping into a mirror. Then suddenly, he exited another mirror ahead of his footballing friend, with the goal in sight.

Amy tossed Crumlish a ball. He weaved with precision, pace and balance between three tightly packed mirrors. Right, then left, before repeating the action like a dog navigating the poles in a Crufts display. Then the inevitable happened, two beasts, both without a ball, were closing in on him, hoping to dispossess the talented player. He froze, then cowered behind the nearest mirror, losing possession.

"Let's go, Crumlish, let's go! Let's go, Crumlish, let's go!"

Jamie, and the children under his protection, may not have been eager to play, but they were certainly having an impact. The voices instantly lifted Crumlish's spirit. His face now wore a steely determined look, and his legs began to move faster than ever before.

He had won back the ball in seconds and was about to take on more opponents. He dropped his shoulder to send the first beast the wrong way. Then with a double step over, he bamboozled the second and left him flat on his face. Crumlish then accurately chipped the ball at his feet into the goal.

Amy dropped another ball from under her arm and smashed a volley goal-ward only to see it agonisingly strike the frame. At her feet, the final ball was flicked up in the air. She launched it towards Crumlish, who acrobatically swung his foot overhead. Leaving the floor completely, he made perfect contact with the ball using a bicycle kick, and he hit the ground just in time to see the ball sail into the net for his second goal.

Amy spied a stray ball rolling near the beast's goal. However, she wasn't the only one with eyes on gaining possession of it. To her left, a beast was stooped and motored towards the ball.

"Ostrich, Amy!" squealed Jamie. "Use the ostrich!"

Coursing through Amy's blood was a small percentage of an ostrich's DNA, and many scientists think this flightless bird has the strongest immune system of any animal in the world. That feat alone forced its inclusion into her parents' serum. Additionally, they have unbelievable speeds. This enormous bird could run at speeds of up to 70mph.

Amy exploded from the ground, leaving nothing but a cloud of dust behind. Her long red hair was a blur as she shot past a stationary Crumlish. In the nick of time, she slammed on the brakes, skidded across the assembly hall floor and tapped the ball into an open goal. Bagging a goal increased the 'humans' tally to three. The skilful pair celebrated with high fives as they returned to their own goal to retrieve a ball and go again. But the celebrations were brief and voided when they noticed the beasts had already put their five footballs into the 'humans' net. The key was to use the mirrors; great football skills could only get you so far. Smart players were the best.

The next attack was not so fruitful. Amy moved too quickly. She lost control of the ball at her feet, and the two under her arms fell away like crisp bags blowing in the wind. To make matters worse, she had seen Crumlish enter a mirror and not return.

Amy called out his name so repetitively and with such panic that her voice was soon hoarse, and only a whisper came out. With the score 7-3 to the beasts, she dusted herself off and limped back towards the goal to fetch another ball. In the corner of her eye, Amy spotted Jamie eagerly watching the game while shepherding the frightened children.

Amy beckoned him with a nod and tossed a football to his feet. Jamie's dribbling was slow and robotic, but he was progressing. Suddenly, without warning or apparent ability, Jamie struck the ball with the inside of his left foot. It ricocheted off three mirrors, between two beasts and into the opposition's goal. 7-4.

What a strike! Amy sprung up from the floor.

Crumlish finally reappeared from a mirror and raced towards the gathered children; Amy and Jamie followed too. "It's that mirror," he said, pointing to a rectangular mirror with an ornate silver frame. "It'll take us outside the hall."

"What then?" asked Jamie.

"We can figure that out when we get there," stated Crumlish. "For now, let's get away from these beasts."

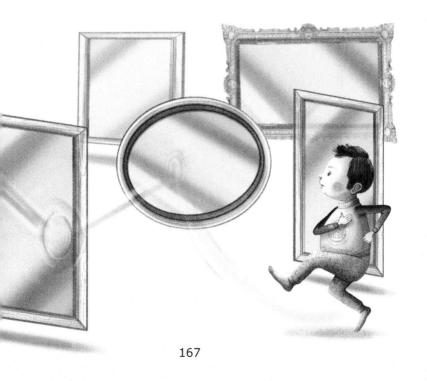

"Right, everyone hold hands and come on," ordered Crumlish.

The children formed a human chain, grasping hands with one another. White knuckled, they headed towards the mirror. Crumlish led the line with Amy, then Jamie, followed by some very resistant young faces. It was clear to Amy that the horrible memory of being ripped from bed and taken into a mirror away from their family was still fresh in each child's mind. She fought against the resisting pulls and yelled to them over the hum of the mirror ball game continuing around them.

"This will get us home, trust me, come on!"

One after another, they all slipped into the mirror and disappeared out of sight.

26
Balloon Fight

Once clear of the assembly hall, Amy assumed line leader and began leading the children through the school corridors. Like a cautious snake, they hugged the grimy walls and slithered towards the exit.

However, every straight stretch of open corridor was greeted with ferocious speed. Pelting on, their legs burned, and their lungs were on fire. Fearing the beasts would be close behind, Amy didn't let up. She hauled the children along faster than many of their short legs could carry them.

"Keep moving," she yelled. "Nearly there!"

She was just about to yell directions when she was interrupted.

From the darkness, a long hairy finger was thrust into her face.

"Shhhhh," said a voice.

Amy's heart thumped painfully. She gulped and squeezed Crumlish's hand so tight he yelped.

The line halted with frightful suddenness, sending everyone into the person in front; like a set of knocked-over dominoes, they all stumbled forward. With no one in front to break her fall, Amy fell to the cold floor to find a pair of black boots before her.

Not a beast but a human. She slowly climbed to her feet. The Reflectionist! A tall, disguised figure stood before her. Dressed in black overalls, an oversized hood and donning a black mask, he looked like the same mysterious figure she had seen when first going to Jamie's house in the Reflection. She could now see the theatrical mask closely. It was a dull matte black with three semi-circles for the mouth and eyes. She recognised those brown eyes, but the voice was muffled beneath the mask.

"Grandad?" she ventured. "How did you..."

"Get to the library," replied the figure. "Now!"

The sound of a beast's footsteps pounding the hard-tiled floor stopped Amy from pursuing any line of questioning. With the hairs on her neck standing on end, she clenched her fists and slowly turned around. The vile creature turned the corner and came into sight. His devilish smile exposed glistening sharp teeth. But more worryingly, he wasn't alone. One by one, beast after beast, they menacingly turned the corner to stare down the human escapees. At least twenty beasts now filled the width of the corridor. The terrifying herd was five or six deep, and with every passing second, more beasts joined the attack.

Every child froze on the spot. The colour vanished from their crimson cheeks, leaving them frighteningly still like statues. Amy took a trembling step forward and reached for the Reflectionist's hand.

"Argghhh," she screamed, touching not a hand but a beast. It fell away from the individual and hit the ground. Amy looked down to see part of a beast, a large hairy toe!

The swarm of beasts padded forward, their eyes wide with fury and hunger. Amy took a step away from the Reflectionist. Only then could she see him removing a backpack and thrusting both arms in to withdraw handfuls of what looked like water bombs.

"Quick!" the Reflectionist yelled. "Help me!" He tossed a filled balloon towards the beasts. It appeared to fall short of the target, instead clattering into a light dangling from the high ceiling. The tennis ball size balloon exploded instantly, spraying the oncoming beast with a glittering liquid.

Reflective dust! thought Amy. No beast dared step into the deadly waterfall cascading down towards the filthy floor. They waited before continuing their advance.

Amy raced towards the water bombs and, in a flash, picked up two. She lobbed one with her right hand and the other with the left, both without even looking, followed by two more, then another two. Jamie was first to race over and help. Soon all their arms were flailing like windmills and tiring fast. Despite the intermittent scream from a beast that turned tail and retreated, the mass pressed on and closed the gap between them and the humans.

"Come on," screeched Amy. "Everyone, come on!" She took the backpack from the ground and rolled the contents towards the cowering children. "Throw them!"

Crumlish grabbed a little rubber balloon and hurdled it towards the beasts. Direct hit! Spurred on, the other children began to step up, and soon the school corridor was filled with glittering water splashes and a multicoloured rainbow. Slowly the beasts were forced back until only a few remained.

But as Amy watched the Reflectionist reach into his backpack and produce a solitary balloon, she knew they were out of ammunition.

"Take this," said the Reflectionist, thrusting the poison pistol Crumlish had dropped earlier into Amy's hand. "And get to the library. **Hurry!"**

The figure bent down for the beast's toe and forced it into a holster around his waist. *Lifford's toe, it had to be Grandad!*

"I'll hold them off. Now go!" he ordered.

Amy ran towards the front of the line, yelling as she did so, "The library! We need to get to the library."

Following a route Amy and Jamie knew only too well, the group were soon surrounded by hundreds of books. The room had remained undisturbed; usually filled with wonder and magic, it now resembled a nightmarish tomb. The room was in darkness save for the glow from a fire exit sign above the door.

Centred in the room stood an unfamiliar object for a library, as large as a door with a delicately designed ornate frame, an anywhere mirror!

"Is that the missing one?" asked Crumlish, gawping.

"The stolen one you mean, yes!" gloated Amy. "My..I mean, the Reflectionist must want us to use it to get home."

"How does it work?" asked Jamie, circling the mirror.

The remaining children stood huddled together, staring at themselves in this unique mirror that could apparently take them home.

The cold glass of the mirror was beginning to steam up with the panting breaths of the frightened children.

Jamie wiped the mirrored glass with his sleeve, "I thought we were going home. Come on then, how's it work?" he asked again, impatiently, in Crumlish's direction.

"That is how it works," Crumlish smiled. "Wipe it. Write where you want to go."

"Let me try!" Amy placed her hands on the cold

silver frame and moved in. She expelled a long warm volley of air at the mirror, making it cloud over again. Then she wrote the words Tarabally Town in the condensation.

As the words faded, the reflection of the group was replaced with a bird's eye view of the town.

"Now what?" asked a little boy who sat crouching at Amy's feet for a better view.

"Right, what's your address?" she asked the boy.

"17 Spring Rock Road."

Amy breathed on the mirror again and wrote the address. As the words cleared, the view of the town zoomed down onto the boy's home.

He gasped and stood up to grab Amy's hand. He began bouncing on the spot.

"What's your name?" she asked the boy.

"Henry," he replied, a smile awkwardly stretched across his face.

Amy clouded the glass again and finally wrote 'Henry'. But as the name cleared, the mirrored glass became black and scorched.

The heroic girl tilted her head back and sighed aloud.

"What's wrong?" asked Jamie, sprinting from the door. "Can't you use it? Is it broken?"

Tears began to follow; whimpers and sobs filled the silence.

"The beasts must have broken Henry's mirror," interjected Crumlish.

"So, they couldn't be followed," Amy added excitedly. "Of course."

She stretched the hair band around her wrist and then released it to snap, "Ah ha!" She breathed on the mirror again, then wrote 'mum and dad'.

"Look, Henry!" she announced. "Is that your parents?"

The sight of Henry's parents in their bedroom came into view. His mum was on a laptop, and his dad was searching a pile of newspapers, their bulging eyes suggesting they hadn't slept from the moment their only son had been taken. Between them was a little girl, sleeping soundly.

"Yes, that's them," spluttered Henry. "And Charlotte!"

"Come on then," said Crumlish, offering out a hand.

"Don't forget, Henry, cover your mirrors when you get home!"

"Or better still, break it," smiled Jamie.

Crumlish, Amy and Jamie passed a smile as little

Henry stepped into the mirror. Once in his parent's room, Crumlish released the clinch and pulled his arm back into The Reflection.

Amy's heart swelled with joy as she watched the sheer ecstasy and uncontrollable emotion displayed in the scene they all viewed through the mirror. Suddenly the scene vanished like a television being switched off as Henry's Dad approached the mirror and threw it to the ground.

Tears streamed down Amy's face as she stepped forward and asked, "Who wants to go home next?"

It wasn't long before only the three unlikely heroes remained.

"You can go first," stated Jamie.

"Well, I was hoping we could go together," suggested Amy. "Remember, my Grandad has removed all the mirrors in my house."

"Ah, of course. Well then, you'll have to come to mine," insisted Jamie.

Amy nudged her friend and smiled, "Let's go."

The three took hold of one another's comforting hands, wrote on the mirror, and climbed into Jamie's parents' bedroom.

27
A Reflectionist Uniform

It was just before six o'clock when Amy reached home, her feet wet from the morning dew on the grass. She sat with Crumlish on a cold concrete step at the rear of the house. The sun was peaking over the rooftops, spilling onto her face. She smiled when she thought of their heroics and how proud Grandad would be.

Amy craned her neck to see Mum's curtains were still drawn, but Grandad's room was already basking in the sunlight. Then again, he hadn't been to bed. *He'd been in The Reflection too. Hadn't he?* She peeked through the kitchen window, checking the coast was clear before entering and sneaking back into bed.

She used the spare key under a rock to get in, and then they stole upstairs as silently as humanly, and as beastly, possible.

"Watch that stair," she whispered to Crumlish as they neared the top of the flight.

The heroic duo crept into Amy's room to find it empty. She thought Grandad would surely be back, already pacing the floors and waiting. She darted into her grandfather's room to see that it, too, was vacant. The bed was already made, and a set of black overalls was folded neatly upon it. Amy grabbed the clothing by the shoulders, allowing it to roll open to its full length.

"Look!" she said, turning to Crumlish. "Do you know what this is?"

"I do. It's a Reflectionist uniform," he replied, poking the sequinned letter R on the breast pocket.

"I knew it was him! *He* stole that anywhere mirror, and he fought the beasts."

Amy threw the black overalls over her shoulder and raced to her room. Crumlish splashed onto the bed as Amy closed the door and stared at her face in the mirror. *It was clouded with worry. Where is he?*

It then dawned on her. The mirror!

"This mirror hasn't been covered!" she stated.

Crumlish sat bolt upright. "Maybe your Grandad took the towel off, waiting for you." He paused, stood up and approached the mirror. He drew a deep breath and began, "You don't think maybe, you know, maybe they got him? I mean, we did escape pretty easily. Perhaps this was Emperor Cashel's plan all along."

Amy gawped, dry-mouthed, and her stomach clenched. "No!" she finally said defiantly. "Look, the mirror isn't clouded over; it isn't broken. They didn't take him! He went himself."

"Himself?" Crumlish asked, befuddled.

"Yes, himself. Think about it; he's the Reflectionist we saw. He had Lifford's toe. That's the beast's touch he needs to get through to the Reflection."

"That would explain a lot. He clearly knows what he's doing then. He'll be fine," Crumlish replied briskly.

The sunshine creeping into the room was suddenly obscured by dark, ominous clouds that rolled into sight. Amy shuddered as sharp rain smashed against the bedroom window. The sky turned grey and angry, and rolling thunder converged on the house. But there was no lightning. No illumination. The sky stayed dark and gloomy. Amy's bottom lip quivered a little.

"I get the feeling he's in trouble. We need to go back!"

"Are you mad? After what we just did! The Emperor will be fuming. All the beasts will be. We helped nine children escape. They'll want revenge on us now too!"

Amy didn't reply at first. She sat motionless and silent, staring at the mirror. Suddenly she popped up as if she had been electrocuted. There was a glint and a sparkle in her eyes. "So, let's give it to him," she said through gritted teeth.

"What do you mean?"

She felt for the poison pistol in her pocket and began climbing into the oversized Reflectionist overalls. "Remember you were about to tell Emperor Cashel who I was.."

"I...I...wouldn't," he stuttered. "I mean, it wasn't my.."

"It's okay. Because that's exactly what we are going to do."

28
Bait

Amy stepped into the mirror again. Hand in hand, she and Crumlish began their path towards school.

A low thick fog whipped around their legs as they apprehensively slithered along the meandering footpath leading to the school gate. The building was now in complete darkness, adding only to the unease weighing down on their shoulders.

"It should be easy to get in unseen. The beasts usually sleep through your daytime, preparing for tomorrow night."

"When they'll take even more children," grunted Amy. "But I think that plan may have changed, especially if they've got my Grandad. Look, Crumlish, let's finish this once and for all!"

Amy led the way once the pair entered the school and quick-footed it towards the principal's office.

"You know, Amy, this would be the perfect time to go invisible. Sneak around the school and find your grandad. Then we wouldn't even need to see the emperor," whispered CD.

"Not this time," she replied confidently. The determined girl held her head high and strode on, exposed but prepared. "Take me to him!"

Just as Crumlish lifted his trembling arm to knock on the door, Amy grabbed him, "Be brave, and stick to the plan."

Crumlish timidly tapped the door with his knuckles; even still, some flaking wood fluttered to the ground and dirt exploded from the surface. The door swung open slowly, with an eerie scream from its hinges. He entered alone and swung the door behind him. It didn't close completely, allowing Amy to listen and steal the occasional glance.

Emperor Cashel didn't turn around to speak. He stood fixated upon the scene outside of his window. "I believe you have a little present for me."

Crumlish swallowed; it was hard and dry. "Well, you see, Master, I.." he began in a trembling voice.

"Did I ask you to speak?" snapped Emperor Cashel without raising his voice. "It has taken me fifty years to track him down, fifty long years. But now he's old and sloppy. I knew I'd eventually catch Charlie," he spat out the name like poison. "He has taken too many of my brethren, so many of your own brothers, and yet, you continue to help these humans."

"He killed the last Emperor fifty years ago, didn't he? Is that why you want revenge so bad?" interrupted Crumlish.

"You rambling moron," barked Emperor Cashel. "You really are a disappointment. I don't care that he killed my brother. It just meant I became Emperor sooner," he smirked, looking down and spinning the orb dangling around his neck. "That one human, Charlie," he spluttered. "He started The Reflectionists. Passed on his knowledge, and now they've killed hundreds of beasts."

I knew it, thought Amy. Her inside glowed with warmness in the cold chilly surroundings. Grandad was even braver than she could ever have imagined.

"I couldn't let him get away with that," continued Emperor Cashel. "And nor should you. And yet you persist on helping that human, his family and the Reflectionists." The Emperor spoke slowly and purposefully. He glided around the room like a cold shadow. Crumlish and Amy, at the door, listened attentively.

"I've never killed any beasts, I swear."

The Emperor loomed over and pressed his face so close Crumlish could taste his breath. "I hope for your sake not. But you have been working with The Reflectionists. You think I don't know about the library earlier. Using my own Anywhere mirror. Thank you, by the way, for leading me straight to it." He flashed a snarling smile revealing his sharp, blackened teeth. "That was fine, though, because while you and your

Reflectionist friends were rescuing the children, my feeders stumbled across what I have been waiting fifty years for."

"Charlie," blurted Crumlish.

"Yes, Charlie. Precious Grandad Charlie," he purred. "We found him stumbling around searching for his grandchild. Another vile human, no doubt."

Amy, only an earshot away, gulped. An icy chill tickled the back of her neck. He does have Grandad!

"To be honest, I'm a little disappointed. He's nothing but a frail old man. I would have never caught him so easily before. But you see, his standards slipped once Charlie retired as a Reflectionist. He stopped moving around. He started getting close to his family. And that was his biggest mistake."

"I have..s...something for you," stuttered Crumlish.

"I know," said Emperor Cashel. "But what good is one human when you helped a whole group escape? I will let the other beasts decide what will be done with you."

Crumlish's voice trembled as he tried to reply, "I'm sorry about the other children. But I needed to rescue them, to get her to trust me. I was always planning on bringing her to you, Master, Charlie too."

"Stop your grovelling and move," boomed Emperor Cashel, banging his tail off the wall and shaking the room. "I can't abide a grovel. What are you babbling on about?"

"Look!" Crumlish staggered towards the door and hauled Amy in. He gave her a reassuring nod.

Emperor Cashel stood looking out the window with his back to the pair. But suddenly, he became very still and started frantically sniffing the air. He slowly turned around, baring his teeth like a shark about to attack.

"I know this child. I know her smell. And what is that?" He began creeping slowly towards Amy, his soulless eyes growing darker still. "Is that Reflectionist clothes I see on you, child?"

"It's Charlie's grandchild," interjected Crumlish. "It's Amy. I was getting her to trust me. And it worked. That's how I got her here so easily. I would have brought Grandad Charlie too with a little more time, Master."

"So, this is Amy Cupples, the fearless child who would return to save her grandfather," drawled Emperor Cashel. He stooped over and sniffed the girl's red hair.

Amy gasped for air, almost suffocating, but didn't let it show.

"Like her old grandad Charlie, I see. Look at the eyes. Look at the rage. I can sense the blood boiling in her veins," he added, running a sharp claw nail over Amy's pale face. "This one is special. You did well, Crumlish. She could have proven difficult to capture. Look at her! Charlie has obviously begun training her early." The emperor, without warning, flicked a finger against the sequinned R letter on her chest, sending her tumbling to the ground.

From the filthy floor, Amy noticed a little smile on Crumlish's face as he received his compliment.

The defiant girl brushed herself off and stood to her feet. She piped up, "You won't get away with it, you, you, horrible monster."

"Why thank you, I do try," Emperor Cashel laughed. "And child, I have already gotten away with everything. Give her to the Saggarts. They can lock the brat up, away from her grandfather," he ordered Crumlish. "When our fellow beasts awake from their slumber, we will feast and celebrate."

This isn't the plan. This isn't it at all. Where is Grandad? I need to act fast.

"Go, give me to the Saggarts. Two idiots. I'll escape again anyway, easy," she snorted.

"Perhaps, child," replied the emperor. He stared intensively at the girl. "Crumlish, you finish the job.

Take her away. Lock her up!"

"Yeah," chimed in Amy. "You're too frightened to lock me up in the classroom with Grandad. You know we'd escape and come back for you!"

"Ha, your Grandad is in the cleaner's store, you fool!" Emperor Cashel smashed his frightening tail against the floor, sending a tremor through the room. "Get her out of my sight!"

29
Transformation

"Wait!" demanded Emperor Cashel. "Come here!" He beckoned Crumlish closer with a horny outstretched finger. "I believe you have redeemed yourself."

The emperor twisted open the mirrored orb that hung around his neck and tipped some reflective dust over Crumlish's head. Whispering a command, the human before him slowly changed.

Amy stared open-mouthed. Every hair stood on end, and her eyes were nothing but white.

She watched as a wave of goosebumps rippled across Crumlish's body. His dark hair began to quiver and his eyes bulged. Pulling at his throat in desperate gasps for air, Crumlish fell to his knees and curled into a ball. He screamed out in pain, then suddenly released a satisfying sigh and climbed to his feet. He discarded his human clothes that had ripped at the seams and looked down at the transformed body and the huge hairy feet that supported his weight. His skinny black legs bent at the two knee joints, and he stood over a foot taller than before. Crumlish slowly looked around the room and caught his reflection in the dirty window. Amy was aghast as the grin on Crumlish's face grew wider still.

"Now, that leaves only one beast pretending to be human," said Emperor Cashel. "Lock her away, and then return to me. We have much to discuss. You have been a lost, stray dog in the wilderness for too long, and it's time you rejoined the pack."

Crumlish pulled Amy by the arm, making her wince in pain. He clearly didn't realise his strength as a beast. His eyes grew wide and shocked when he caught sight of his tearful friend.

"Sorry," he whispered meekly.

"Don't be, my beast," called the emperor. "You're one of us now. Look at the fear in the child's eyes now," he chuckled.

Crumlish held his head high and avoided eye contact with Amy. He forcibly marched her along the corridors towards the cleaner's storeroom in the belly of the school.

Amy sensed a change in her friend and not just his appearance. She looked him up and down, trying to comprehend his beastly form and convince herself that he was the same person.

"So far, so good," she ventured. "We know where my Grandad is. Let's get him and get out of here." There was no reply. No eye contact was even made. "Things haven't changed, right?"

Concern grew with every step taken in their muted conversation.

The school was silent, save for a faint but persistent tapping sound. In the darkness, ahead of the duo, a figure emerged. Amy gulped down. It was hard and dry. It was a peculiar feeling to see nothing and be frightened of everything. Drawing nearer, a beast appeared. Hunched over and shuffling forward, the beast gave a nod of approval to Crumlish as they crossed paths.

"Did you see that? Did you? I wasn't ignored or treated like an outcast."

His voice sounded the same, and as he glanced down at Amy, she could see that even his innocent, sweet eyes were the same. But she could tell that in just that moment, that little bit of acceptance and attention was more than Crumlish had received over the last fifty years. Amy gave a little grin and nodded with uncertainty.

Bearing in on the tapping sound, Amy pulled free from Crumlish and raced on. She heard a faint but recognisable plea for help at the locked store door. The rasping voice cut through the thick fire door like a hot knife through butter.

"Hurry up, hurry up! That's Grandad. Open the door, Crumlish!"

There was a deadly pause. Wearing a vacant look on his beastly face, he finally shuffled forward like an old-aged pensioner in a post office queue and forced open the door.

Grandad was cowering at the back of the dimly lit room, banging his walking stick against the wall and clinging to a solitary torch that flickered just moments from extinguishing.

Amy bolted inside, "It's me, Grandad! It's me."

Grandad climbed to his feet and hobbled to his granddaughter. Amy planted her face into the old man's chest. The colourful silk pyjamas felt nice on her cold red cheeks. *Pyjamas? Not black overalls, no hood, no mask and no toe belonging to Lifford. Wasn't he the Reflectionist?*

"I came looking for you, my child," he sniffed. "Now they've got us both."

"They don't, Grandad; we've come to rescue you," she smiled. "Let's go!" She took her grandfather's cold hand and moved towards the door.

Crumlish slowly closed the door as the two humans approached. "I am sorry," he whispered.

Amy quickly raced over and wedged her foot in, "What are you doing? This isn't the plan."

"I know, Amy. But I can't go through with it. Look at me. I'm a beast again. And if I disappoint the emperor, he'll kill me for certain."

"Look, Crumlish, just open it, don't have me use my powers. My strength could burst down this door in seconds."

In an instant, Amy recalled a dung beetle's ability to pull weights 1000 times their own body weight. That's like a human pulling six double-decker buses.

"Maybe you can, maybe you can't," replied Crumlish. "But you won't. Not in front of your Grandad Charlie. He doesn't know about your abilities. And I don't think he'd appreciate finding out you've kept a secret from him."

Amy grunted and threw a fist into the door.

"I'm sorry, Amy. I have to do this," said Crumlish. "It's not like I can run off and hide in the human world now." He tried to force the door closed.

"OOooowwwww," screamed Amy, refusing to move her foot. "But you are better than this. I know you are. I have seen you be better. Remember how happy we were when we rescued the missing children? Think of how good you felt. You're a good person, I know it. Don't give up, not now."

"But I'm not a person! Look at me. I'm a beast. I'm from The Reflection, and I need to stick with my own kind for my safety."

"Yeah, but what about our safety? Please don't do this," Amy sobbed, tears streaming down her face.

"Please forgive me," Crumlish pleaded, finally forcing the door closed. The room suddenly fell into darkness, and the torch died.

30
Don't Stop Now

Crumlish collapsed against the door.

"I can still hear you," Amy yelled. "You're crying! I know you don't want to do this."

She suddenly fell silent upon hearing thunderous footsteps approach. Crumlish pulled himself to his feet and shook his face dry.

"Tears of…"

"Joy, we assume," finished the second Saggart, standing behind his twin in the narrow corridor.

"Now there's a face we," began the first Saggart.

"Haven't seen in a while," said the second.

Amy glanced over her shoulder at Grandad before willing the stress in her body towards her ears. She held her breath and listened with intrigue, like a wolf, who in the open, can hear sounds from as far away as ten miles.

"You got us into trouble," the Saggarts said in unison.

"Ahh, sorry about that," Crumlish replied. "Part of my plan, you see. It's all fine now, sure, look at me. I'm back in favour with master. I even got my beast body back."

"Good, at least we can look at you now."

"Without feeling sick." The Saggarts both released a deep, hearty laugh.

"Are you going to the feast later?" asked the first Saggart.

"I hear it's to be the biggest and best one ever," said the second Saggart, popping his head over his twin's shoulder to be seen.

"It is?" asked Crumlish, already knowing why.

"Charlie is on the menu. And his grandchild, the little girl who looked like you."

"Looked like me?" quizzed Crumlish.

"Yes," answered the second Saggart. "When you were a human. She smelled like you too."

"All those human children look the same if you ask me," continued the first Saggart.

"She wasn't scared of us enough, though," added the second.

"She's like me," repeated Crumlish.

"Well, she was," laughed the first Saggart.

"Not after tonight," boasted the other Saggart before both beasts lumbered off.

Amy continued to listen as she heard four gigantic feet move away and footsteps grow faint. But Crumlish didn't move. He was stationary.

"You see!" Amy yelled. "Some beasts and humans are alike; you and I are the same. The little differences are nothing to the big similarities."

She called out his name again into the face of the door, "Crumlish!"

Amy could hear breathing. It was long and deep and echoed down the narrow corridor. And then the sound of heavy feet on tiled floors charging towards the door.

Crumlish flung open the sealed door as if it were non-existent and stared apologetically at the girl and her grandad, "I am so sorry. I just didn't know what to think. I have never been too good at making decisions. That's probably part of the reason I was turned human in the first place."

"I disagree," said Amy, squinting her eyes. "You always make the right decision in the end. Now, let's go!"

"Let's go?" interrupted Grandad. "With a beast?"

"It's Crumlish, Grandad."

The old man stared intensely, then rubbed his eyes, "Oh, so it is. Well, what are we waiting for then?"

From the silence, a piercingly loud scream echo shook the school. A sound Amy had never heard before, high, blood-curdling and eerily final.

"Stop!" cried Emperor Cashel, whipping his tail around the corridor walls, sending plaster and bricks raining down.

The escapees didn't stop. They hurdled on in fear while being mowed down by the emperor. Grandad was moving at a terrific pace, using the walking stick like sports day champions might move in the three-legged race. The enraged chaser was bearing closer and closer. His enormous stride galloped on while the **thump thump thump** of the swinging ruling orb hit against his chest.

"Quick! In here, everyone!" yelled Amy, veering off right through broken double doors, her red hair fluttering as she ran.

"But Emperor Cashel knows about the Anywhere Mirror in the library," called Crumlish.

"I know! We aren't going there. I have an idea!"

31
Staff Room Mirror

Together the trio treaded an unfamiliar path towards the school staff room in The Reflection. The room was equally as vile as the rest of the school. For some peculiar reason, Amy thought this place would be a haven full of secrets and mystery, a place no child had ever entered. But soft cushioned seats were mouldy and rotting and sat in a rectangle around a large stain-covered coffee table.

The smell was more pungent than even Emperor Cashel's breath. With the door ajar and a faint yellow light flickering, casting intermittent shadows across the room, Amy quickly found the smell emanating from the fridge. The tiniest hum from the appliance regretfully drew Amy closer, making her gag.

"Come on," Crumlish said wearily as he clambered towards a large square mirror above the sink. "He's close."

"Precisely! He's got to follow us. He's got to go through this exact mirror, too," pressed Amy. "Wait... wait...wait..."

The staff room door was thrown open and the emperor strode in. The calculated girl made eye contact with their foe for a brief second. "Okay, go, **go go!**" she rushed.

Crumlish was in the middle of the three. One hand was in Grandad's and the other was pulling Amy towards the mirror. One by one, they slipped from Emperor Cashel's view.

The real staff room was nothing like its Reflection counterpart. It smelled beautiful, with fresh fruit, air fresheners and cleaning products. The surfaces gleamed, the wooden floor sparkled, and each chair looked more appealing and comfortable than the last.

Amy scanned the room and its display walls. Not full of teaching secrets, control techniques, or a list of potential troublemakers; instead, it was dates, times, meetings, targets and evaluations. All colour coordinated and all extremely boring. She couldn't help but be disappointed.

"What now?" pressed Crumlish. "He's coming!"

Amy headed towards the door and the rest followed. They fell into a wide-open corridor, the type any child sent on an errand couldn't help but sprint along. Every inch of the wall, on either side, was filled with children's work- art displays, stories, tips on recycling and an 'under the sea' mosaic.

"Wait for me down there," ordered Amy, pointing at a glass cabinet at the end of the long corridor. "Make sure he can see us!"

Amy zig-zagged her way towards Grandad and Crumlish, darting from side to side, to every socket in the wall, armed with the little water pistol filled with poison. She eventually panted up to join the group when finished.

"What were you doing?" asked Crumlish.

"Motion sensors," explained Amy, shaking the empty plastic toy. "I'm sure you've noticed the smell. This building is covered in them. I replaced the air freshener with some poison. Now we've just got to wait."

The group stood stony still and kept a watchful silence upon the staffroom door at the opposite end of the corridor. They didn't have to wait long. As expected, as planned, it slowly opened.

"This is it. The moment he passes one of those plugs, pssstttttt! It will be all over. He will melt away into nothing."

"Genius, my child! Genius!" whispered Grandad. "I knew you'd make the perfect Reflectionist. And you already look the part." The old man squeezed Amy's shoulder as he beamed.

"Ahh, Charlie," Emperor Cashel bellowed. "How is this to greet an old friend?"

Amy was perplexed further still. *Old friend?*

The emperor took one step forward. They all smiled a little. He stepped on a little further. Their smiles grew bigger still. As he was about to take his third and potentially final step, the group were salivating. But then he stopped. Emperor Cashel stepped backwards, turned around and unfurled his tail to point at the wannabe heroes. Then he retreated into the staffroom and out of sight.

32
Mortal Danger

"I think he's gone," said Crumlish, finally easing his grip on Amy's forearm.

Looking into the corridor's emptiness, Grandad took a long breath and explained, "Not this beast. Not now, not when he's so close to revenge. He won't give up that easily."

"Come on then," urged Amy. "We need to move."

Together they scurried along the corridors, checking each door they passed. A familiar guilt was beginning to burn in Amy's tummy. Her plan had been a flop. The poison was wasted, plugged into the wall beyond use, and now they were running for their lives through a vacant school with no way out.

"Look, a computer room," said Grandad. He frantically began pushing the door with all of his might. It was teasingly being forced open. But suddenly, they were thrown under a sinister shadow. Darkness befell the group and their bodies tensed. They looked to the ground and the enormity of the shadow stretching out before them. Its shape was undeniably recognisable. Nobody turned around to confirm their belief.

"Run!"

They galloped off again, even quicker than before. Moving with such haste was proving as difficult for the emperor as Crumlish. The clean, shiny tiled floors offered no traction under their padded hairy feet. Their legs spun like a hamster wheel, not going anywhere. It reminded Amy of when she tried to run on ice; turning corners was nearly impossible.

Amy grabbed hold of Crumlish and hauled him around each corner. She herded them all into a room, the girls' toilets, one she knew had a broken lock that never worked. They all stood huddled in the centre of the room, sinks and mirrors on one side and cubicle toilets on the other.

"Crumlish, keep guard," Amy said sternly.

He begrudgingly moped towards the broken door to peek out.

The minutes felt like hours, as is always the case when you wait for something bad to happen, or something good for that matter. Amy tucked her hair behind her ears and nervously twisted the hairband still hanging around her wrist.

The agonising silence made the tense situation only worse. Despite fighting the urge, their heavy eyes were beginning to close. Grandad made his way to one of the low sinks. He leaned his walking stick against the wall and splashed cold water around his face. He stared at his reflection for an unusually long time. When he finally turned to face the rest of the group, he sat on the sink. It cried out under his weight.

"There's only one thing for it," he started. "It's me he wants. So, it's me he'll get. Amy, I want you to make a run for it. Set off the fire alarm; that will draw some attention and get out!" He turned then to Crumlish. "I need to ask even more of you, my oldest friend. I need you to hop into this mirror," he said, pointing behind him with his thumb. "and lure Emperor Cashel here. Tell him I'm alone and waiting. If he wants his revenge and is brave enough, tell him to come and get it."

"No Grandad, no way!"

"The mirror!" pointed Crumlish.

"Yes, this mirror. Well, any of them, I don't mind. Just get him here," replied Grandad.

"The mirror," quivered Crumlish. "The mirror!"

Grandad's eyes flickered between the two pairs staring back at him. They had grown wide and fearful. Amy slowly raised a trembling finger to point, "Move away from the mirror!" she screeched.

A sudden feeling of mortal danger crept over Grandad. In the corner of his eye, he caught sight of the emperor's pointed tail. But it was too late, and he knew it. With a lightning-fast whip, he was snatched and held aloft in the crook of the tail. Grandad was suspended high in the air, controlled by Emperor Cashel as if he were nothing but a puppet.

The rest of the emperor confidently sprouted out from the mirror. Crumlish and Amy looked at the intimidating creature with craned necks. His open mouth twitched with anger, revealing his horrid, jagged teeth and the tips of his rotting, brown gums.

"Well, well, well," he said crisply. "What do we have here? My favourite people all gathered together, how convenient. Stop squirming!" he barked at Grandad, whose eyes were bulging and his hands frantically pulling at the tail locked tight around his neck.

Amy never took her horrified eyes off the emperor. Terror-stricken, Crumlish took a step nearer to the door.

"You're a brave girl, foolish but brave. However, I can already smell the fear growing inside you. I shall enjoy feasting on you tonight, as well as your grandfather. I'll blend you both up into a nice succulent stew." Emperor Cashel turned his attention to Grandad swinging helplessly in the air. "Finally, we meet again, Charlie," he spluttered. "This has been a long time coming. And I don't intend on rushing a thing. Funny, isn't it? When you retired from being a Reflectionist, you stopped killing my beasts and began killing yourself. It was a matter of time before I caught up with you," he chuckled. "It has taken fifty years, Charlie boy, but I shall enjoy finishing you and your little band of Reflectionists, once and for all. Every beast shall celebrate tonight, of that there is no doubt."

33
Another Beast?

Emperor Cashel was drooling with evil intent as he glared at the group with piercing eyes.

"If I see you move towards that door again, Crumlish, I will end you first," he barked with venom. "Now Charlie, what would you...." He paused. Crumlish took another sly step.

In one sweeping movement, the emperor threw Grandad into the air with his tail, caught him in his enormous hand and swiped his tail around, smashing Crumlish against the wall. Clumps of plaster, brick and paint cascaded down onto the escapee beast. He lay motionless before groggily clambering back to his feet and shuffling towards Amy. The girl crouched down to huddle next to the trembling Crumlish.

"Now, where was I? So, Charlie, what would you do in my position?" he asked, returning his attention to the suspended old man whose neck was enveloped with a hand.

"I'd never be in your position," he panted.

"Humour me. What would you do if you were betrayed over and over again? It wasn't good enough to kill hundreds of fellow beasts with your Reflectionist band, but Emperor Dungloe. He may have been an annoying brother, as you know, but he was still a brother nonetheless." Emperor Cashel was menacingly circling the group while swinging Grandad like a puppet.

"Let my Grandad go!" Amy screamed in anger. Her voice quivered as she slowly rose to her feet, a little faint with fear.

The emperor paused. He raised Grandad higher still, then craned his enormous frame toward Amy. "As you wish." His putrid breath blew Amy's hair back.

Suddenly Grandad was released and fell fast towards the ground. Without even a look behind him, the callous emperor swished his tail again and snatched the elderly man up before he hit the ground. He walked away, chuckling.

"Stupid, stupid child! Your Grandad?" he laughed. "You know nothing. Haven't you told them, Charlie? Haven't you told anyone?" He began tossing Grandad around freely. With each jolt, some of the chocolate Maltesers fell from his pockets and one slipper fell off. "Look, little girl, your Grandfather is.."

"My Grandfather is a Reflectionist, the first Reflectionist. I know that," beamed Amy.

"What's that?" interrupted Crumlish, pointing to another mirror above a sink.

A beast's foot was slowly emerging from the Reflection, first was an enormous hairy toe, perfect for silently padding up to a child before snatching them. But it was followed by a human hand. Next, the long dark sleeve of a pair of overalls poured out from the mirror. In moments a masked man was climbing onto a sink and into the girls' toilets. He surveyed the room and the imminent casualties before him.

It's the Reflectionist! Wait, so it couldn't have been Grandad. Amy's eyes flickered towards her grandfather and the look of surprise on his face.

The tall, gangly figure proudly brushed down the embroidered R on his breast pocket and jabbed the beast's toe into a holster around his waist. He raced towards Crumlish, brandishing a clear bottle filled with what looked like beast poison. The figure grabbed Crumlish from behind with one arm, and the other was raised above the beast's head, threatening to pour the poison. Amy's eyes widened, and her short panting breaths quickened.

"It's okay now," yelled the stranger from beneath a mask. He turned his gaze towards the frightened and confused eleven-year-old girl, "Don't worry, Amy, it'll be fine now."

Amy's overwhelming surge of hope was interrupted by the emperor, whose tone seemed pleased with the actions of the Reflectionist.

"Oh no, don't hurt my accomplice," Emperor Cashel yelled mockingly. "Whatever would I do without him?"

Amy noticed a peculiar sarcastic tone to his response.

"Yeah, well, drop the old man, or this beast gets it," demanded the masked Reflectionist.

"You don't have the guts. You Reflectionists are nothing but cowards, invented to make worthless humans feel a bit safer. Go on then," urged the Emperor."If you think you're brave enough. Use all your poison on him."

Amy jumped up like a Jack in the Box, "Don't! He's good. He helped us."

"Ha," chortled Emperor Cashel. "That's what I wanted you to think. He's evil, like all beasts. But you'll do nothing about it."

"Oh, I will. I'm brave enough!" boasted the Reflectionist. He then emptied the entire contents over Crumlish and stepped back. The Emperor's uncontrollable laughter shook the room as he salivated at the sight before him. But nothing happened. Crumlish didn't melt away, disintegrate, die or vanish. He just got wet.

The Emperor was more crestfallen than the masked stranger. "Useless. I thought your poison was deadly."

"So did I," the man replied solemnly. His eyes behind the mask revealed that he was now more frightened than anyone in the room. "It's meant to kill evil beasts."

"But I'm not evil," insisted Crumlish, shaking himself dry. "I've been helping."

"I told you he was good," interjected Amy. "And now we have no poison."

"Pathetic!" spat the Emperor. "I'll deal with that cowardly beast myself after I've drawn this little family reunion to a close." There was a smug smile around the corners of his mouth. Then he stretched his mouth wide, revealing his sharp teeth and the absolute blackness at the back of his throat. Slowly the cruel Emperor moved Grandad towards the jaws of death.

Amy's eyes glazed over as she looked straight ahead at no one or anything. Grandad glanced towards his granddaughter. The moment he saw a flash in her glassy blue eyes, he knew she had a plan.

34
Flying Chocolate

Amy slowly reached the floor and picked up a little chocolate ball that had rolled to rest against her foot. Ever so cautiously, she made tiny movements, free from Emperor Cashel's gaze. She removed the hairband from around her wrist and stretched it between her thumb and index finger. She placed the little poisonous treat precisely in the middle of the band and cocked it back with her other hand like a catapult.

"Do it, Amy," screamed Grandad. **"Do it now!"**

Emperor Cashel foolishly swivelled his neck towards Amy. She released the little brown bullet towards his enormous gaping mouth. The Malteser spun violently as it raced towards its intended target, flying clean past the teeth and straight down the back of the throat.

"Great shot, sweetheart," yelled the masked man excitedly. "Bull's eye!"

Amy couldn't see his face but could tell from his eyes that he was grinning. She was now certain who the mysterious Reflectionist was.

Without warning, Emperor Cashel dropped Grandad and began grasping at his throat. "What did you do?" he screamed. "It stings, it burns, what is it?" The emperor collapsed to his knees with a clatter and began panting. His eyes were now level with Amy's, and she didn't look away.

"It was poison. You know, the kind you said didn't work. We aren't so useless after all, are we?" She pointed to the embroidered R on her breast pocket and, remaining straight-faced, watched the merciless emperor writhe in pain.

Emperor Cashel began rolling, rocking and rattling around the tiled toilet floor. His tail whipped about like a fishing rod cast into the sea and his body flapped like a fish out of water. With a distinctive long lanky stride, the mysterious Reflectionist flung himself at the child and old man, grasping them both at once.

"Amy, my darling," he sobbed. "You're so brave. The bravest." He ripped the mask off and frantically kissed every bit of the skin on the girl's beaming face.

"Dad," she gushed. "Grandad, look- it's Dad," she added, pulling her grandfather closer.

"I know, Amy," he smiled. "I've always known."

"I'm so happy you two are safe," said Dad. "What were you thinking? Rushing in to save the other children is my job. I would never have forgiven myself if anything bad had happened to you."

"Where were you then?" asked Amy, trying to justify her decision and make sense of everything.

"I was getting the Anywhere mirror. But by the time I got to the room for the children, you had all gone. Thank goodness I found you all in the corridor. Without you, I would never have been able to throw so many balloons and fight the beasts back. You'll make a wonderful Reflectionist someday," smiled Dad.

"By someday, you mean today, right?" replied Amy with a grin. "So, I assume you were never in Costa Rica. Does Mum know?"

Grandad interrupted before Dad could reply and ushered the pair away from the Emperor. The reaction was much more wondrous than anything they could have imagined. Emperor Cashel was starting to balloon up. But balloons rarely stay inflated for long. A hissing sound emanated from somewhere near his head. As he shrank, his body quivered all over with tiny waves and ripples. Then the spinning began, first clockwise, then anticlockwise, like he was in a washing machine, all the while barking like a sea lion. His insides then vanished, like someone had taken a vacuum cleaner and sucked them clean out. His empty hairy skin fell to the ground like dirty clothing.

"Well, that's that," announced Grandad. "Let's get home." With his words still hanging in the air, the old man was already moving towards the exit.

"Look, look!" screeched Crumlish.

Clouds of glittery dust plumes rose from the emperor's hissing remains. It danced like a swarm of bees before shooting into the vibrating ruling orb that lay abandoned on the ground.

"What was that?" Amy asked.

"Reflective dust, it joined the orb," Crumlish replied, his dark beastly eyes fixated on the trembling orb. "Remember the chant? Dust from the Reflection…

"Past Emperors are thee, Heed my words and listen to me," interrupted Amy.

"Exactly! Any moment now, that orb will fly off to its new master, the new emperor! And no doubt he'll want his revenge too."

Dad exploded up like he had been electrocuted. From the moment he was on his feet, the excitement grew inside him. Twitching and hopping on the spot, he reached for his mask and looked poised to race off.

"Where are you going, Dad?" asked Amy.

"I need to follow it, my love", he stated. "I've got to stop the new Emperor before he even starts."

"You're leaving us again?" she asked. "Already?"

"It was never my choice, sweetheart. I had to. Your Grandad needed me. He's too old to do it by himself anymore."

Strangely Grandad remained muted. He was sweating profusely, and his eyes bobbed between Amy's and the vibrating orb. Amy stared hard at him. There was a frightened look on his face. One she'd never seen before.

Dad crouched down and took Amy's delicate fingers in his hand. "If the beasts knew where to find a Reflectionist's family, it would be the end for them too. That's why I couldn't tell your Mum. I only left to protect you. And I couldn't come home until the job was done, couldn't risk a beast following me." His eyes twinkled, and Amy found it impossible to be angry with him.

"Yes, yes, Amy. Best to let him go," Grandad rushed. "Go on, Patrick, get you into that mirror and be ready."

The old man took his hand off the door handle, sighed and ran back towards Amy and her dad without a hobble. He quickly withdrew Lifford's toe from Dad's belt and thrust it into his hand.

"Here you go. You go get him. I'll keep Amy safe. Sure, you know I will."

The orb suddenly shot up and floated suspended in mid-air.

"Quick," rushed Grandad. "Quick!"

Dad wheeled away. Stopping, he lovingly looked back at Amy. She couldn't help but return a smile. As Dad motioned towards the mirror, the emperor's ruling orb began to quiver violently. Everyone held their breath. Silence befell the room save for the dripping tap on the last row of sinks.

"Get out of here," urged Grandad. "Patrick, leave!"

Dad had one foot in a sink and the other in the mirror. However, he stopped when the orb flashed around the room in a blur. The sound of the buzzing motion shook their very eardrums. The pattern was peculiar, zooming this way and that. In a room lined with mirrors, the orb still hadn't left. It chaotically roamed, appearing lost.

Grandad shuffled towards the exit.

Suddenly the orb froze, suspended five feet from the ground. Then it whizzed towards Grandad and the door.

"Shut the door, now! The orb's trying to escape!" yelled Amy.

But Grandad didn't close the door. Instead, he threw it wide open. The orb, seemingly with a conscience, ignored the gaping escape and floated stationary, waist-high in front of Grandad.

The old man brushed down his grey hair and looked solemnly at the three staring him down. He then slowly opened his hands, revealing his rough, coarse palms.

Light from above danced off the orb as it spun violently, smothering the room in a whirling light. The orb abruptly halted, then rocketed into Grandad's open hand.

"I knew it!" blurted Crumlish. "I just knew it!"

Dad climbed down from the sink and grabbed hold of his daughter again.

"I guess I've got some explaining to do," said Grandad, smiling nervously.

The End

Printed in Great Britain
by Amazon